Bourbon Decay

Donna Jolly

Screen Porch Press

Published by Screen Porch Press
Copyright Donna Jolly 2006

Cover Art by Mandy Horn

First paperback edition, March 2006

Printed in the United States of America

Acknowledgements

Several people supported my efforts in the writing and publishing of this book, and I would like to acknowledge their contribution. Thanks to Andy for encouraging me to cast my net wider, and a special *gracias* to Sean for his input. My pal Robby is always encouraging me to take "seeds of the truth" and amp them up a few hundred watts. Is this what you had in mind, Robby? To Carla, you're such a larger-than-life person that you inspired those seeds in not one but two characters. Though this is a work of fiction, I'd like to thank my grandparents and my parents for being just crazy enough that I was inspired to create this story. Finally, Roger, you've endured more than your share of my writing habits (and a lot of other bad habits) over the years and you deserve a special literary award for spouses.

Chapter One
Rockets and Holes

I spent my childhood searching for innovative ways to run away from my family. I built rockets to the moon made from wood and metal scraps I found in Grandpa's work shed. Mama and Grandma wouldn't let me play with hammers for fear I'd bang myself up, so I stacked things to create my rockets — pieces of boards, sticks, plastic buckets, bricks. My creations were rockets as an abstract, but in my heart I believed I would actually succeed in building one that worked. I was so proud of these creations that I carved my name into the wood with a rusty nail. Lisa Tingle. The letters were large and bold.

With equal fervor, I dug holes to China with a little red sand shovel and pail. My dog, Dino Martin, helped, getting in the spirit and digging along with his long black and pink nails. If anyone had asked me why I wanted to go to China or the moon, I would have shrugged. Given the way things were around our house it could have been my own variation of "I think therefore I am." I became aware therefore I wanted to run away from home.

With the advantage of age, I can, of course, articulate the reasons that led to my strong desire, and there were many. In general, I can't remember ever feeling like I belonged with my family or even in our town, where everyone knew everyone too well. We lived at the frayed edge of the Old South, in the late 60s. The old dusty ways were yielding to a lighter, more hopeful time. Most people expected a newer, better world, but in Newitville, Mississippi, the scent of change could never break through the stench of complacency and ambivalence. And in our house those smells were so thick I could take a bite out of the air.

The problem started before I was born. My parents, Belle and Rodney Tingle, did not expect me. In fact, Mama had been expecting menopause, as she was just hitting middle-age and prone to always assuming the most dramatic. I'm not sure if they were happy she was pregnant. My sister Ava was ten when I came along and already her true colors glared. She suffered from poor grades because she couldn't quit daydreaming about boys and romance. Mama said she was comatose with desire.

Like Ava, I, too, had my daydreams. Mine consisted of shiny rockets and deep holes. I imagined peeking my head out on the other side of the world, and seeing a Chinese person staring at my blonde self, blinking at me in wonder. I'd drop down the hole and begin a new adventure, believing someday kids would read about me the way I read about Pippi Longstocking.

At the time of this particular phase, I blamed my desire to run away on my aunts and teenage cousins. They created much turmoil in our household. Mama's widowed sisters, Teckla and Pie, would bring their offspring to our house nearly every day each summer to see my maternal grandparents who lived with us. Grandma gave Teckla and Pie extra attention, feeling bad because they were too young to be widows, even though they seemed pretty old to me

Mama did not extend the same kindness. As soon as her sisters arrived, she usually retreated into her private sanctuary, her and Daddy's bathroom, which doubled as their wet bar. Grandma and Grandpa didn't like Mama and Daddy drinking because alcohol was "ruining the world." Alcohol caused communism, Civil Rights, prostitution, divorce, cancer, spider veins, and anything unjust, illegal, deadly or unpleasant.

Every night, while Grandma cooked dinner in the kitchen, my folks had "Happy Hour" in the bathroom, which they had turned into a Vegas lounge. Sinatra played from a portable phonograph, and the lavatory became a wet bar. Mama purchased little martini shaker printed curtains for the one small window. Each night, she sat on a black vinyl bar stool while Daddy sat on the lime green toilet, lid down. They drank Jack Daniel's and ginger ale highballs.

Grandpa and Daddy didn't speak to each other. To this day, I don't know all the many reasons why. As Mama would say, "It's a long history." But they stopped speaking so long ago that well into their old age, they themselves had honestly forgotten what made them stop in the first place.

There was only one thing that was for certain: Mama hated her sisters' daily summer visits, partly because it was her house too and no one ever asked if they could come over. Their presence impeded her drinking, even though she hid in the bathroom. She had to be careful not to get drunk or her sisters would make a gargantuan deal out of it and embarrass Mama in front of Grandma, who in turn would start in with her disparagement against Mama's favorite pastime.

Teckla and Pie liked their cocktails as much as my parents did, but around my tee totaling grandparents they were as sober as Baptists. My aunts took this act to extremes by gossiping about people around town who drank. "I heard Myrtle Fell was at the post office drunk. Her hose were down around her ankles." Pie said one afternoon, in a typical tattle about one of the town's numerous drinkers.

I looked up at Mama, who had been examining some frozen meat Grandma had put in the sink to defrost. She picked up the meat like it was an object from outer space. I think she wanted to feel useful and cook, but didn't know what to do with the red ice block in her hands.

Grandma shook her old jowls slowly as she listened to Pie's story, a cocktail of disapproval and sadness stirring in her eyes. "I just don't know why these damn fools drink." She gave Mama a look, who looked back as if to say, "Oh, na-uh, don't start." Mama walked out of the room in a huff, her intentions to cook dinner forgotten as she retreated to her bathroom/bar for a drink.

On most of these visits, while Mama contended with her sisters and mother, I would be outside furiously building rockets or digging holes, anything to get away from my sister and cousins, who would soon find me and start mocking me for being a little kid.

Quinn, the oldest, belonged to Teckla. Quinn never went anywhere without Lester, Pie's oldest. Mama claimed that neither Lester or Quinn were "right in the head" because they were "queer." I didn't understand what she meant by queer, of course. I thought she meant they were weird, like the deformed potato from Grandma's garden that resembled

George Wallace, the former Governor of Alabama. Knobs and tumors on the potato resembled his hollow eyes and liver lips.

I did find it unusual that two young men lived at home with their parents and hung out with their younger girl cousins — they were a good bit older, old enough to have been discharged from the Navy, for reasons none of the adults ever mentioned.

Next in age came Aunt Pie's oldest daughter, Carson. She wanted to be a writer. She wore hats over her long blond hair as well as silky dresses that flowed around her thin legs. Her favorite expression was "What the Faulkner?" It was an expression she used instead of "What on earth?"

Then came Delia, Pie's youngest. Satan invaded her dreams in an attempt to steal her soul. She prayed often. Sometimes, she broke into prayer in the middle of a conversation. It unnerved everyone in the family, even Grandma.

Of course, there was my big sister Ava, who did not eat, period, unless it was Grandma's peach cobbler. Then she ate the whole plate. To this day I cannot tell you what Grandma's cobbler tasted like; I never got the chance. Since Ava ate only this, the adults allowed her the whole thing. I got my hand slapped if I so much as sniffed it.

Ava always wore new clothes, pressed and perfect. Her hair, every strand, knew its place. In old photographs of me, my clothes are mismatched and I have wild-child hair, ratted all over. I had the disheveled look of a child raised by a pack of gorillas. My mother and grandmother, for whatever reason, did not participate in my grooming. I got baths, and Grandma combed out my wet hair. Mama sometimes reminded me to brush my teeth, but that was the extent of it. Ava somehow inherited the gene that propelled her toward a finished look. I needed a manual, some encouragement, or peer pressure; the latter would thankfully come in my teens and save me from going through life with mismatched socks.

Ava and Delia had the religious bond in common. Angels sat on Ava's bed at night and laughed at her, she said, because she prayed to God to bring her a cute boyfriend to marry. In fact, that's all she prayed for, and she believed that it had backfired. She hung posters of Paul McCartney on the wall and often asked Daddy what time it was in Liverpool. I think it made her feel guilty that she was so obsessed with Paul McCartney and not concentrating on more worthy pursuits. Hence the laughing angels sitting on her bed.

The youngest cousin (next to me) was skinny Van (Teckla's baby). He delighted in tormenting me and the others let him. He was eight years my senior, but you would have thought he was a full-grown adult. He taunted me with things like, "You're about as smart as a cork, aren't you?"

The remark didn't ruin me as Van may have hoped, because he, and all my teenage cousins, were genuinely boring. They liked to sit around and talk about other kids their age, or the Beatles, and tell jokes I didn't get. In fact, "Get it" was one of their favorite sayings. Someone would finish a story and end with "Get it?" And then they'd laugh. Their laughter had a vicious unity to it. Every time they cracked up over something funny, it reminded me of the time the whole family was over for dinner, and Grandma had set up a buffet on the table. Van put his hand under my plate of spaghetti and slapped it upwards, tipping the whole thing on top of me. Everyone thought this was so very funny, especially Mama who couldn't conceal her mirth over seeing her little one dripping with noodles and sauce.

There are defining moments in all our lives, and at that moment, I understood that I was the youngest, the baby. I lacked development, skill, any art of maneuvering. My awkwardness and gullibility created joy for the others. Some other child might have felt empowered for being able to change their moods, but that joy made me understand that I was different from them, a difference that made them feel superior.

My desire to get away from my family intensified the summer before I started kindergarten. It's when I finally understood and could articulate that my aunts and cousins were only part of the problem. It's as if I had suddenly hopped up on a cliff far away and could see the whole convoluted unfortunate picture of us. My parents and grandparents deserved most of the credit. Some may say it was Jack Daniel's fault. But if a dog is bad, do you blame it or the owner?

I stayed home with Grandma and Grandpa during the day, while Daddy rode around town in his Tingle Air-conditioning Sales and Repair van. Daddy fixed Newitville's broken air-conditioning units that struggled in Mississippi's swampy hot air, feeble heroes fighting a valiant cause: cooling Hell. Mama was a ticket taker for the Confederate Museum, a homage to the Civil War housed in a century old courthouse.

Pie and Teckla came over daily that summer. They would bring the teens, who would take over Grandpa's old Studebaker by sprawling across it on blankets under the scorching sun. They reminded me of pictures I'd seen of panthers in Tanzania or somewhere, plopped over the limbs of trees. Some of the teens sat on the hood, Ava liked the roof, the boys usually relaxed on blankets on the ground right by the front grill.

One particular unpleasant memory stands out from the others that summer. It's the day I decided to never let my annoying cousins bother me again, because I had my hands full with my Mama, Daddy, Grandma and Grandpa.

It started out as usual. Teckla and Pie brought the teens over. They lumbered across the Studebaker while I hid behind a rock pile on the far side of the yard and dug a hole to China.

Mama returned from work early with a headache. Seeing all her sisters with their kids there yet again was more than she could handle.

"I just want some peace," she shrieked. "For God's sake, this is my house, can't you people ask before you come over?"

"This is my house, too," Grandma screamed, "and my Goddamned kids can come over any time they want! They don't have to ask!"

"You have always been jealous of us, Belle," Teckla said.

"Ever since you were a child," Pie agreed.

We could hear them clearly even though we were outside. The teens hushed and laughed quietly, amused as another private joke flapped around their group. I even stopped digging my hole. Already, I had uncovered earthworms and fragments of green and blue bottles. I had dug up a small chicken bone, which Dino now gnawed on.

After more shouting, which ended in Mama sobbing loudly, Grandma stormed out of the house, the screen door banging behind her.

"Pack up the car, Quinn. Take the kids to the Battlefield. And take the baby with you."

There wasn't enough room for me in the car and Quinn told me to pick a lap. I chose Carson's. She smelled like Dentyne. "I'm going to write a short story about your mother," she announced looking at me with her spotted green eyes. They looked like small green mirror-balls, speckled with blue and gold.

"It will be an epic. 'Who's Afraid of Belle Tingle?' Get it?" she asked the others. No one got it.

Quinn stopped at the Phillips 66 so we could get snacks: crème wafers, Dr Pepper and Saltines. I liked the Battlefield, a Civil War national park sprinkled every half-mile or so with large monuments of soldiers in battle, or charging with Dixie flags and rifles raised high to heaven, or generals on rearing horses. Each statue bore an inscription about the "brave dead" who "fought valiantly" for their beliefs. And each monument was dedicated to a state, including Yankee ones. The plaques even had nice words written about the Yankees, which made me suspect that the world was meant to be civil and nice, and that my family violated the natural order of life.

My favorite place in the park had to be the Illinois Monument. It was a domed marble rotunda with many stairs leading to its entrance – a stair for each day the Yankees terrorized Newitville in the bloody siege.

Once inside the monument, you could look straight up and out a hole in the top to see the sky. It never rained inside, and Daddy had told me the structure was an architectural marvel. The wind circulating at the opening blew the rain out and over the outside of the marble roof. Brass plaques covered the walls, bearing the name of every soldier from Illinois who died during the Siege.

Quinn pulled into the little parking area at the monument and I scooted out of the car and ran ahead, happy to have a few moments alone, knowing the teens would take their time getting up the stairs. I walked inside and went straight to the wall to carry out a ritual. I liked to touch the names of the dead soldiers and imagine their lives. I let my fingers linger over the names and I had the most peculiar feeling, similar to the time I walked in on Mama sitting on the edge of her bed, crying into her hands.

"What's wrong?" I had asked her.

"Nothing," she said after a minute. "Go play."

I did as she said. Mama seemed so deep in her misery that I thought it might spread.

And it did. I grew sad just thinking of the moment. I pulled my fingers away from the names of the Yankee dead, and decided to endure the teens tormenting me in exchange for crème wafers. I found my cousins outside the structure, stretched out on a worn baby-blue blanket Quinn kept in the car trunk. They were eating, laughing, sipping their colas and ending sentences with "Get it?"

I sat down. Van asked, "Who said you could join us?"

"Oh let her be, she never talks," Quinn said.

"That's because she has nothing to say," Van said. "She ain't the sharpest hatchet in the tool shed, you know."

I glowered at Van, but then, as if to prove his point, I scratched my head and stuck my finger in my ear. I did this for no other reason than it was something to do; it had become a habit of sorts. I walked back over to the monument. I wanted to sit against the marble and take a nap, deciding the crème wafers weren't worth listening to my cousins after all.

"Oh we hurt the wittle brat's feelings," Van baby-talked.

"You've teased her enough," Delia said. "I need to pray harder for you, Van. I really think Satan is inside you." She made the sign of the cross in front of Van's face and he slapped her hand away.

"Shut-up, you Bible-thumping God-squad minion."

"Don't be blasphemous. God hates that."

"Can we elevate the conversation?" Carson said, her voice ripe with the type of misery I'd only heard from my mother when she pleaded for a little peace around the house. "Just make me laugh. All I want is to laugh. Lester, amuse me. . ."

I moved just far enough away that their barbs sounded like an inaudible buzz. The heat from the sun toasted the marble of the monument. My eyes grew heavy. A wind trickled over the hill.

Evidently, I nodded off because I woke a bit later, the sun still high in the sky. I heard sad accordion music drifting up from the woods. The sound made my hair stand up on end, and I imagined that the music was a sad melody played by a Civil War soldier ghost. I got up, drawn to the music.

Carson yelled after me, "Hey, where are you going?"

I ignored her, not that she or any of them cared. As the oldest girl, she probably thought it her duty to ask. Lester and Quinn ran after me. Lester yelled over his shoulder, "We'll keep an eye on her. A walk in the woods might be fun. Maybe we'll see some old Yankee bones."

But they ran past me into a thicket of trees, as if they were following the music, too. I went around back behind the monument and stared at the line where the tall oaks and pines began. The accordion was louder there. The music came from nowhere and everywhere, the notes had hitched a ride on the breeze.

Somewhere in those woods, I knew a Civil War ghost stood over a campfire and played the mournful tune. I stood at the tree line, wondering if I should go inside the woods and see the ghost. I knew they existed. Grandpa had told me that ghosts liked the woods; it's where they went when they weren't haunting, he said. Like snakes, they didn't really like people, and they could hide in the trees.

I guess I never stood still long enough to listen or hear one till now. And now that I could hear the ghost's tune, I figured, what the Hell, be brave. Be Tom Sawyer. Go in the woods.

Of course, I was just as afraid of slithering slimy snakes as I was of ghosts, so I stepped carefully, watching everything, the ground, the trees, the bark, the limbs overhead, the leaves sizzling in the breeze. The accordion music grew stronger and I followed the sound to where it seemed to come from. I heard a noise, a twig break, a tinkle of what could have been either laughter or ice crackling in a cocktail glass and I turned left, down a slight hill where a large boulder sat like a freak in church. Two large oaks framed the landscape, covered in twisted vines and laced with trailing red-veined ivy.

I saw Quinn on his knees at the bottom of the hill. A low lying branch partially blocked my view so I couldn't see what he was doing. Something was off, and for a wild moment, I thought Delia's religion had overcome him and he was praying. If it could get a rascal like him we were all doomed to be devoutly religious. I had images of me as a Catholic — like Delia— wearing a veil on my head, praying in Latin, smelling of candle wax.

I moved closer, stepping carefully, afraid of ghosts and snakes, and as I did, I saw Quinn fully. His pants were pulled down around his ankles. Something ugly and purple stuck out between his legs and by the jerking motions of his hands, it looked like he was trying frantically to pull it out. I thought he had been stabbed by it, that this thing must have fallen from the highest hidden branch overhead. Then I remembered Ava telling me once that boys looked different than girls down there. They looked pretty ugly, I thought, and Quinn must have hated it too because it looked like he was trying to get rid of it.

Lester just stood there, close to him, and watched.

"What are you doing?" I asked, and both boys jumped. Lester moved away fast, like he had just touched a hot stove eye.

"Quinn got bit. He's just trying to squeeze out the poison. That's all you've seen. Don't go telling the girls, they'll just panic."

And that's what I did, panicked. I forgot immediately that boys were supposed to look different down there. My fear of snakes overcame me. Lester hadn't said what bit Quinn, but I figured it surely had been a snake, hiding out in the woods with the accordion-playing ghost. I turned and started running. I had to save the day. I had to help Quinn. I ran hard, fast, forcing my short, gawky self to make quick time against the air rushing past me. My legs moved beyond their capacity, my lungs tingled and burned, singed from my efforts. Somewhere in the back of my mind, I saw a future scene, with my family giving me more respect because I was a hero.

Breathless, I ran up to rest of the teens, still lounging on the blanket. "A snake bit Quinn between his legs and now he's trying to squeeze out the poison! And Lester was just standing there doing nothing!"

They all stared at me. Ava with her hazel, bored eyes, Carson, through her Carson-speckled daze, Delia, searching my face trying to comprehend, and Van, always a step ahead, cool, malevolent. He laughed, tossing his head back.

"Now that is too funny. A snake. Poison!"

Delia said, "Shut up, Van, this is not good."

Ava said, "She's making this up. Just ignore her."

"Oh she ain't making this up. She saw what she saw. I told ya'll Lester and Quinn were funny that way," Van said, "but no, you can't comprehend such things."

"What the Faulkner? If you are right, Van, this is all very Tennessee Williams," Carson said. "Thank God! Finally, someone in this family has done something other than be an alcoholic."

I screamed, "QUINN HAS BEEN BIT BY A POISONOUS SNAKE AND HE'S GONNA DIE! WE HAVE TO GET HIM TO THE HOSPITAL!"

Suddenly I felt strong arms reach from behind and swoop me up like a tornado.

"We told you it was nothing to worry about," I heard Quinn say. He set me down with such a thud that unbalanced, I fell and rolled down the hill like a cola bottle. I blacked out at the bottom and woke a few seconds later to the sun slapping my face with its heat. Sad, lazy accordion music drifted from the woods, taunting more than before. The teens laughed. The music drowned their voices. Over their shoulders, a high white cloud moved frothy and slow, shaped like a boot. It floated toward Van's head and looked like it would kick him. I laughed at it, drool sliding out the side of my mouth.

The music faded and I could hear Van say, "You are such a little moron. Look at you, lying there, laughing like an idiot."

"It is a tale told by an idiot," Carson said. "Get it?"

No one got it.

"I was just taking a piss," Quinn said and laughed. "Just a piss in the woods."

Lester matched his merriment. "Oh boy, we got you good. We told her there was a snake coming out of his legs, shooting out venom."

They hooted; I tried to talk. "That's not what you said." It came out, "*Blegh*."

Ava said, "Why did I get stuck with you? You are such a baby. You will believe anything, and then you can't even get the story right." Then she looked around, a quizzical expression clouding her eyes. "Where is that accordion music coming from?"

"There are houses through the woods," Lester said. He pointed. "The park property ends back there in that thicket of trees."

"Ghosts." I did not mean to say that word out loud. They laughed. Van made haunting sounds and I thought about the lonely dead Yankee in the woods, wishing he'd come out and scare the daylights out of him.

"Let's go home," Carson said. She had wadded up the blanket and tucked it under one arm, and grasped the package of crème wafers in the opposite hand. "Fun's over. I'm bored."

Quinn and Lester stayed behind while the others got in the car. I did not move from my spot on the ground. Lester leaned down, his face inches from mine, and said, "Don't bother getting up if you are going to tell that little story to your folks when you get home. We'll just leave you alone out here with all the snakes in this park. Do you know the Battlefield is home to more snakes than any place in the world?"

"That's right. You can stay out here and be raised by snakes. You can eat slugs for dinner." Quinn tugged at his belt.

"Leave me alone." I finally managed to form a complete sentence.

"Fine. We'll go," Quinn said. He turned to Lester. "We'll teach that little brat a lesson."

They walked away, leaving me there on the ground. A moment later, Quinn started the car, and as he drove past me, Van leaned out the back seat window.

"Poor little baby, living out in the Battlefield with the snakes."

They stopped the car at the end of the parking lot. I couldn't see it, but I could hear the engine idling.

"Come on. Your Mama might have another breakdown if we left you," Quinn hollered from the driver's seat.

Van, imitating my mother with a high-pitched, affected voice, mocked, "You could have at least asked me if it was okay to leave my baby in the battlefield! My God, doesn't anyone care what I think?"

I stayed on the ground, allowing the burning sun to panfry me. The teens didn't care; it added to their bored amusement.

And with that realization, I decided to get up and get in the car. I'd go home, but only so I could return to digging holes to China and building rockets to the moon. I was willing to endure the teens once more because I understood now why I always dug and built. I wanted to get away from them, as well as the adults. They were all either mean or crazy or both. They were mean to me and to each other. Grandpa and Daddy didn't speak to each other and they ignored the fights of the women around them, with Grandpa hiding in his tool shed tinkering on things long beyond fixable, and Daddy hiding in front of the TV, getting lost in variety show comedy sketches. Grandma was mean to Mama and Mama was mean to her sisters and to Grandma, and everyone was mean to everyone. We kids had inherited it. We preyed on the weak. And being the baby, I had weakness covered in spades.

So I knew now. I knew why I was driven to spend so much time getting my scalp burned under the sun, feverishly building inventions of escape. I did it instinctively, like a salmon swimming upstream to mate. I had just never thought about why. But now I understood my motivation and with the knowledge came a clearer determination. I had things to do, holes to dig, rockets to build. I had to get away.

Chapter Two
One and Ten

Had it not been for my father, I would have no doubt tried my hand at running away, even if I only ran as far as the school playground about a half mile down the road. I adored my father because he so clearly adored me. Not that the others in my family didn't. Daddy, though, took a special pride in my odd proclivities like digging holes. He'd walk up to me in the backyard where I would be digging a hole and beam.

He'd say something like, "That's just the cutest thing I think I've seen yet." He didn't mind that I was a tomboy. It made his world all the better. God wouldn't give him a football playing son, but he'd give him a little girl with dirty fingernails and a penchant for spitting.

At the start of my fifth grade year, Daddy gave me a slim pocket-sized book called "Football for Girls." He wanted to make sure I fully understood what was happening on the playing field whenever we watched an Ole Miss Rebels' football game.

Sometimes we'd drive up to Oxford to see them play, but more often we watched them on WJTV out of Jackson. I could have known nothing about football and still loved Ole Miss just for the colors of the team, red and royal blue. There was also the whole Rebel experience: the band playing "Dixie," the Rebelettes marching their immense, dazzling smiles across the field, and the fans waving their little Confederate flags at every Rebel defensive tackle or offensive yard gain.

The book fueled my inherent Rebel love. I learned about passes and penalties, rushing, blocking, and the difference between a linebacker and a running back. I stomped around the house yelling the Ole Miss cheer, "Hotty

Toddy, Gosh Almighty, who the hell are we? Hey! Flim Flam Bim Bam Ole Miss by Damn!"

The more I fell in love with Ole Miss, the more Daddy's affection for me bloomed. I could make his face light up even when I did mundane tasks like drying the dinner dishes Mama had washed.

"1 and 10, do it again," I'd say, and wrap a towel around another plate. Daddy, who would be sitting at the table reading the evening paper's sports section, would look up with a silent "Aw shucks" on his love-smitten face.

That year, Ava did something that made Daddy love me even more. She was a high school senior and rather than concentrating on good grades or her future, she spent every single night with her obsession, Lewis Mitchum, a darkly handsome high school dropout who'd held sixteen jobs in the last year. They had just become engaged and threatened to marry the day she graduated. Mama and Daddy walked around the house lamenting what to do if "The girl goes through with it." Their dismay made marriage seem more like murder than a journey of love.

In contrast to Ava, I looked like the embodiment of hope. Daddy would ask me, "What do you want to be when you grow up?" and I'd say as I had for years, "An Ole Miss cheerleader." He would beam brighter and larger than any father had ever even thought of beaming.

The more he loved me, the more I became obsessed with learning more about him; in particular, I wanted to learn the secrets his Navy chest could reveal, the one he kept padlocked at the foot of his and Mama's bed. It had the metal smell of a gun.

I'd say, "Daddy, open that trunk."

And he'd say, "Doodie, now you don't want to see what's in there." "Doodie" was my nickname, given to me by Daddy. I would be in my thirties before it dawned on me what my nickname meant.

"Come on, Daddy, open the trunk I want to see."

"Aw, no you don't."

It would go on like this till he would turn red and flap his jowls and say, "Well I ain't opening it and that's that" Then I'd say, "Why not," and he would throw up his hands and trundle off to the living room to lose himself in some TV show.

I believed that he could not bring himself to open the chest. It held a mystery he did not want uncovered. Maybe it was photographs and letters from his own father, a man who died before I was born. Maybe it hurt too much to see these things — reminders of his loss. Or maybe he had a fortune sleeping in there, waiting to take it out when we really and truly needed the money, like right before we all starved to death or something. Perhaps he didn't know what the contents were. Some magical being had given it to him and told him never to peek inside. My skin hummed with all the possibilities.

There was only one way to find out. I would have to trick him into telling me.

One night after watching Fred McMurray on "My Three Sons" tell Dodie a bed-time story to help her sleep, I got an idea. I invented an affliction that would not allow me to sleep. My only cure would be a bedtime story. I believed that if I got Daddy to tell me stories from his past, the secret to the chest would be revealed.

Around eleven o'clock that first night, two hours past the normal time I should have gone to sleep, I announced my need by knocking on my mother and father's door. Mama happily volunteered, practically salivating to read "Snow White" or "Cinderella."

"I want a real life story," I said. I don't think it ever occurred to either of them that a child in the fifth grade was getting past the point of being read fairy-tale bedtime stories. My parents would have been happy if I stayed little forever.

"I can do that, I can tell you a real story." Mama's eagerness grew.

"I want Daddy to tell me a real life story," I told Mama. I poked out my lower lip and lowered my eyes, then coughed a little, childish manipulations that always worked with my parents.

Daddy's body stammered and stuttered. Mama looked at him, pleading. "The child needs to sleep. Children need sleep or they grow up ruined. Ava never slept enough and just look at her. Please, Rodney."

Mama sensed that if Daddy was going to get through this he didn't need an audience. She pushed him toward me and he walked me to my room. I climbed into bed and snuggled happily under my covers, pulling the blanket up to my nose and staring at my father with earnest, waiting eyes.

He sat next to me on my bed and looked up at the ceiling. "Ugh," he said. "Umm."

"Tell me about you and Mama before me and Ava."

"Umm." He sighed and sweated.

I felt bad for him, so I said, "And it has to have Ole Miss in it."

He looked relieved.

I did not expect the story he told.

"When I met your mama, she had one of those bobby-soxer crushes on Frank Sinatra." Daddy's voice sounded like a milkshake tasted. I could feel myself starting to get sleepy after the first line. I pulled the covers up to my nose and peered at him through slit eyes.

They met in what was to become my hometown, Newitville, Mississippi, at a USO dance near the very end of World War II. It took place in the basement of an old Episcopal church. Posters of Uncle Sam and Hollywood stars, like Sinatra, Gable, and Lombard shared wall space with crosses and images of Jesus.

"She liked to sing," Daddy said. And in my head, I heard her singing *All or Nothing at All*.

I closed my eyes and the song and his voice drifted together into a half-dream. "*And if I fell, fell under the spell of your charm, I would get lost in the undertow. . .*"

"She wanted to be another Judy Garland, but the USO and the church choir were the only places her mama and daddy allowed her to sing in public. A good Catholic girl couldn't very well perform in a nightclub, Lisa.

"She sang one or two songs a night. 'All or Nothing at All' was her favorite and, next to Sinatra, I'm telling you, she sang it better than anyone. She learned phrasing by listening to Sinatra's records. But honest, sugar, when you got right down to it, she had the instinct to know that the audience loved a singer with heart."

Daddy paused for so long I fell into a deeper sleep. I was in the USO hall, watching my parents, floating over them in my PJ's, little cowgirls roping an unseen cow.

"Lisa Dorothy Tingle, listen up."

"Mmph," I grunted and opened my eyes a little.

"You know, she put so much of her heart into the words I nearly cried."

The night they met, Daddy watched her and fell in love. He liked her nose, a feature that she hated. It looked French with its slight bump in the middle.

Daddy seemed to be full of all the right things to say.

"Your voice poked a hole in my heart," he said, coming up to her as soon as she finished singing. "And the only way to sew up that hole would be for you to dance with me."

She stepped carefully off the makeshift stage in her wobbly white high heels with frayed t-straps. Without another word, he took her hand and led her to the dance floor. She just followed, watching him watching her.

I could vividly see her over-coifed, coiled brown hair and Daddy in a clean-pressed sailor suit.

Daddy wrapped me so far into her story, the past became present: Even now, I am in the USO hall:

"All or Nothing at All" plays over the PA. A young Sinatra sings like no one has sung ever, as if his is the only way. My parents dance slowly as lovers should, cheek to cheek, hips swishing through the air.

Mama is powdery and sweet from too much Coty; Daddy is scented in lime and gin. A fake silver flask is secured by a leather strap under his shirt. Every few dances, he excuses himself and finds a dark corner to take a few swigs. It calms his nerves around this pretty USO girl, her big white teeth flashing an S.O.S signal for romance.

Daddy is thin; he resembles a hard-living Jimmy Stewart. He has just returned to Newitville from World War II that day, after having recuperated from wounds inflicted when the Japanese bombed his Navy ship. Daddy's left hand and leg got in the way of some shrapnel. It didn't cause any serious damage, but it did leave thick permanent scars on his hands and legs.

As he squeezes Mama's hand while they dance, he knows she is the one, the only one. He senses this is bad, that this kind of want will only lead to his eventual undoing as a bachelor. Yet, being a young man, testosterone or ignorance screaming "reason be damned," he pursues my young, beautiful mother.

The sound of Daddy's voice broke my enchantment. I left the past and was once again back in my room, snuggled in bed.

"You don't know this, but I had big plans for my life, and those plans didn't involve romance. I wanted to go to Ole Miss on the GI plan and play football, though that was a silly idea. I didn't have the discipline for school. I liked having a good time too much, drinking and dancing or playing cards with my buddies," Daddy said.

He leaned down and kissed my forehead. "Good-night, little Doodie."

"Ugh," I said. That was it? He lulled me into a cozy near-slumber with how he fell in love with Mama, then he ended on an ominous tone, that his dreams were shattered by this woman, and evidently, hers were shattered by him as she was nowhere near to being the next Judy Garland. I hadn't even heard her sing except in church along with the congregation. I didn't think her warbled voice was all that good, but she and Daddy evidently put a lot of stock in those shaky notes.

He shut off the merry-go-round lamp on the nightstand and left. I stared at the shadows on the walls, the outline of pecans from the tree outside my window. They looked like tiny footballs.

Daddy came into my room the next night and sat beside me on the bed. I pulled the cover up to my nose and looked at him. I had gotten maybe a couple hours sleep the night before, drifting away only when a light rain came around dawn.

"I'm going to tell you a new story."

"You don't have to."

"No, now I want to help you sleep. It didn't seem to work last night, so I'll talk longer tonight."

"I'm pretty tired."

"Good. Good. That's swell."

This storytelling affliction had started something in Daddy. It was as if his tongue were relieved to be set free. It was a dog's tail, wagging, wagging, so happy to just wag.

"You should know about how we all came to live together," he said, "I've only told you the beginning. You need to know the middle, so you know why things are the way they are."

"How are they?"

"You know. With your grandparents and all."

I wanted to say, "I know, Daddy," but then I didn't. I had just attributed it to the way things were in my family. I wanted to know my father's secrets, though, and why things were the way they were with my family was part of that. But that secret scared me. It meant somewhere, someone did something bad. And I just didn't want to know who or what.

So Daddy began his story.

"When your mama and I were younger, we didn't have any money to speak of, which wasn't really different from any other time in our life," Daddy said. I caught that same ominous tone in his voice from when he ended the last story.

He kept talking, the same odd wistful voice speaking softly.

It went like this: My mother worked as an operator for Mississippi Bell. Daddy repaired air conditioners for Dixie Refrigeration.

My mother's parents ran a farm for the Saint Ignatius nuns. Grandpa liked to drink a bit too much. Sometimes he went through a fifth of whiskey a day. The nuns caught wind of it and around the time that Ava Gardner was conceived, they fired him. My grandparents had to leave the farm.

Economics dictated that my parents and grandparents move in together. Due to Mama's complete frugality, she and Daddy had enough money to swing a loan at the bank. They bought three acres of property outside Newitville on a winding, two-lane road that cut straight through tall pines covering ceaseless ridges. Across the road and up the ways a bit sat a small, squatty, white-framed country church with a black congregation. Mama thought the church made our land a little more sacred.

Daddy and Grandpa cornered off a flat section of the front acre where they would build the house, where Mama and Grandma could have a view from the kitchen window in the back of the state's television tower in the distance. The red glow would be pretty at night.

Neither man was a carpenter. Daddy repaired air conditioners and believed it qualified him to do the electrical work. Grandpa reasoned that since he had been the fix-it guy around the nuns' farm, he could build a house.

Daddy told me that he and Grandpa never had an easy relationship, not even in the beginning. From the start, Grandpa didn't like him much. He said Daddy strutted around like a rooster, cocky, confident, and audacious. When Daddy met Mama, he told a lie. His family had money. Mama married Daddy thinking she was about to become a gloves and pearls lady. His family *had* had money, before the Great Depression. They owned a granite quarry in South Carolina. They lost everything though, and were penniless. His father ran off and his mother took a job as a food server in a high school cafeteria. Mama eventually told Grandpa the whole story, and that started the tension between him and Daddy.

Mama got beyond Daddy's lie, more or less, though sometimes she dug it up like an old love letter from a former lover and waved it around using it against him. Grandpa, however, never forgave Daddy. "I don't cotton to liars," he would say sometimes out of the blue, eyeing my father.

And Daddy didn't like Grandpa. He thought "the lazy bastard" was useless without Grandma.

In a rare act of contrition, Grandpa and Daddy put their differences aside for a common, practical goal: shelter for the family. Both men needed a home for their family, and between them they had barely two dimes to rub together.

On the final day of building, Daddy and Grandpa were resting on the roof. They had just finished nailing down the last shingle of tin — they used tin because they didn't have enough money or credit for anything better than tin.

They sat on doubled-over towels protecting their butts from the hot tin, drank beer, and enjoyed the feel of the sun. There was a moment of peace, when the wind kicked up and hissed through the trees. They looked at each other and almost smiled; or at least they didn't grimace. An electricity passed between them, a feeling of pride over a completed job, a job with worthy and noble intentions: shelter for the family.

The finished product wasn't much to see. The exterior had a sandpaper rough covering designed to look like red brick. The house was slightly larger than a modern-day doublewide trailer. My grandfather and father didn't care about the looks. It was home, their own.

Like so many more good moments to follow over the years, this one did not last. A shingle of tin popped with the rudest abruptness, and then another bodacious shingle followed, and another and another until a whole insolent row came undone.

Without any hesitation, Grandpa blamed Daddy, who in turn blamed Grandpa.

"Why you lazy bastard, I oughta pop you," Grandpa said. He thought about it half a second and did.

"You son-of-a-bitch," Daddy said.

Grandpa shoved Daddy in the chest. "You're the sonofabitch."

Daddy lunged for Grandpa and they wrestled. They immediately lost their footing and rolled off the slant, bumped over the rain gutter and landed straight in Grandma's newly planted rose bushes. Grandma rushed out the back screen door with a broom.

"Sonsofbitches," she yelled, hitting them both with a broom. "Worthless bastard sonsofbitches. Straighten up and act right."

"And we did, for a while. We always did what your grandma told us. She is the driver behind the steering wheel in this family," Daddy told me. "Of course, your grandpa was the damn nail in the middle of the road."

"Is that lie you told the reason you and Grandpa don't speak?"

"It's probably one reason."

"Is that fight you had about the roof another reason?"

"It's probably one reason, too."

Daddy was long on stories and short on answers. I wasn't getting any closer to finding out what was in the trunk, but I had my fill of learning why my family was the way they were.

"I really need to sleep, Daddy." I wanted him to leave, but I also hoped he wouldn't. I was torn between the dangerous portents of his story and the excitement from melodrama. I felt I would be better off just not hearing anymore. I loved my parents, I loved my grandparents. But football was easier to love. Football was only about sweet victory and noble defeat. It was bordered by simple rules. I wanted to see the little pecan etchings on my darkened ceiling again. I didn't want to hear any more of the story.

"I'm almost finished, Doodie."

"I might nod off."

He picked up my hand, his rough skin scratching my palm. "This is a good story; Doodie. It ain't no Cinderella, it's our life, it's real. Someone in this family should be thinking about reality before we end up in our graves thinking, 'Is that all there was to life?'"

I had the covers pulled up to my nose again, and maybe he could see the confusion and fear in my eyes. He pushed himself off the bed and said, "It's late, though. There's too much to tell in one night." He shut off my merry-go-round light and left. The shadows from the tree slowly etched across my ceiling. Little footballs swung in the night breeze.

Daddy's drinking took a turn for the worse. Telling me these stories opened something up inside of him, something he didn't want touched. The following evening, he passed out in his chair before nine o'clock.

He snored, filling the room with the smell of Jack Daniel's. It had a ripple effect throughout the house. Mama cried in the bathtub, bubbles reaching up to her chin. Grandma sat at the kitchen table and read from the bible, mouthing words. Grandpa teetered in his work shed, a naked light bulb showing him his rusted odd objects. He muttered. Ava was on a date with Lewis Mitchum. She came home late as always, and looking pasty, her hair uncoiled.

I believed I had not uncovered the secrets. Only its effects. There was only one thing certain. I had to get inside the Navy chest. I snuck into their room while they watched television and looked at it sitting at the foot of their bed, a big metal guard dog, a place to catch Mama's work clothes when she flung them off, a table to stack old magazines. I touched the padlock and tried to dangle it, thinking it might snap open. It barely moved; it lumbered a little, side to side. I peered through the tiny keyhole and saw nothing, but smelled must and metal. I thought of death, what it must look like, black, still.

I sat in front of the Navy chest and stared. I touched it, put my cheek against the metal, gnawed on the edge, and thumped the lock. I had a true sleeping affliction now; I could not rest until I found out what was inside that chest. I believed Daddy's secrets were at the root of my mother's tears, my grandfather's mumbling, my grandmother's incessant Bible reading. I was pretty sure that he shared no blame in my sister dating Lewis Mitchum, but I could have been wrong.

I went out to Grandpa's work-shed. I thought he could help me. I always had the feeling that Grandpa was on my side, though I couldn't tell you why I felt there had to be a "my side." A line had been drawn in our family dividing Mama and Daddy from my grandparents. Maybe Grandpa thought I belonged to their side. I don't know. He stood over his workbench eyeing a screwdriver he had stuck into a tarnished meat grinder. He looked up at me and said, or rather, grunted, "Needs cleaning."

"I think Daddy has secrets," I said.

"Sonofabitch unions."

"He hides things in his trunk.

"Communists!"

"Maybe you could help me open it."

Grandpa reached into an old Folgers can and pulled out an ice pick. He held it up and stared at me. I wriggled my finger at him and he followed. I led him into the house. We walked passed Grandma sitting at the kitchen table mouthing Psalms. Daddy snored in his chair. Jack Daniel's filled the air. I showed Grandpa the lock on the Navy chest, and as he fiddled with it, I could hear Mama crying in the bathtub in the next room, talking to herself about all the sacrifices she'd had to make in her life. I was so used to it I didn't even wonder what had set her off.

It didn't take Grandpa long to open the lock. He handed it to me.

"Put it back," he said, meaning when I was done with the pick.

"You don't think this is a bad thing for me to do, do you?" I asked. "I mean, a child's daddy shouldn't have secrets from her, should he? I should know stuff."

"Ain't no secrets," Grandpa said. As he walked away, he muttered, "Empty bottles."

As I lifted the lid, the smell of mothballs and must filled my nose. I stooped over, and as the light flooded into the chest, I fell back, startled by the first thing I saw. It was a gas mask with a green pig-shaped nose as the filter. I moved it away and saw scary images in my head: smoky battlefields under a gray sky. In the distance, firebombs lit the thick clouds. Men trudged through ankle-deep mud in pig-nosed masks. I wanted to vomit, anxious but full of curiosity over what I'd find next. I assured myself that my imagination had gotten away from me, and comforted myself with the fact that Daddy had been in the Navy, on a ship in the blue Pacific, not in the Army. He didn't march across battlefields. His boat docked in harbors bordered by coconut groves. Hula girls greeted the sailors with pink drinks speared with paper umbrellas. This pig-nosed mask was surely given to him as a precaution by an overprotective government.

I found a pea jacket next. It was heavy as a gun, heavy as the threat of death, heavy as my love for Daddy. I held it to my face and thought of him wearing it. There was a picture on the living room wall of Daddy wearing this pea jacket, standing on a pier with the Golden Gate Bridge in the background. He had a crew cut and a cleft in his chin. His eyes looked different, the same color, but they belonged to a different person. They looked like my eyes when I saw myself in the mirror.

I slipped on the jacket and almost fell over backwards from the weight. My hands were hidden in the long arms and I could smell faintly the Daddy I now knew. It smelled of Limeboy and Jack Daniel's, but the jacket also had the old-lady odor of moth-balls.

I pushed one sleeve back and picked up a little cigar box, then sat on the floor. Inside the box was a picture of Daddy, much younger, wearing a suit and standing next to a pretty woman. I turned over the photograph. Someone with a very feminine hand had written "Rodney and Helen Tingle on their wedding day."

My muscles nearly went spastic. Daddy couldn't have these kinds of secrets. I had hoped for a tragic but heroic past, something like he had saved his entire Navy ship, but lost his best friend to a nefarious Japanese POW with a concealed gun. Daddy shot the POW, but too late. He blamed himself for his friend's death.

His secrets got worse. I found another picture of another, younger, woman. I turned it over. "Janice Tingle, 1955." The date confused me, until I found the birth certificate folded like a letter. Janice was the daughter of Helen and Rodney. She died of polio, which I learned by reading a sympathy card from one of Daddy's WW II buddies. I put the box away. I folded the jacket on top of it and put the gas mask back where it had been. I locked the box up and wiped sweat off of my forehead. I went into my room and got in bed, curling into a fetal position. I left the light on. I did not want to see footballs on my wall. I did not want anything to make me think of my father.

Eventually, Mama came in to kiss me good night. Her face was all powdered and she wore red lipstick that matched her eyes. She was cheery, real cheery.

She said, "Good night, sugar blossom baby doll cutie pie."

I said, "Tell me a story."

"Should I tell you about the time I met your father?"

"No, tell me about the time Daddy met Helen and how they got married and had Janice, who died of Polio."

I looked at the wall when I said this; I could not bear to see my mother's face. I understood that I had just ripped from her whatever tiny bit of joy she had remaining in her heart. When the silence got to me and I finally faced her, Mama wore a look of defeat.

"How do you know about this?"

"I know things. I find things out."

"Did your grandparents tell you?"

"No, Ava did," I said.

Ava was already in so much trouble for dating Lewis Mitchum that this little lie would not matter. They were beyond talking to her. Also, I had just laid a trap to find out if my sister had knowledge of Janice and Helen.

"That child is not right in the head, telling you these things."

"So she knew and I didn't."

"You're too young to understand. That's why. We'd eventually tell you."

"Tell me now."

Mama scooted away, as if the truth required distance. "Your father married too young, right before he went to war. Helen got pregnant, and after she had the baby, she fell in love with another man and divorced your father while he was overseas. That's one reason we are so upset about your sister dating that worthless Lewis Mitchum. We're afraid she'll make the same mistake your father made and have to get married."

"Why did he have to get married?"

"I'll tell you when you're older."

"Tell me now."

"It won't make sense."

"Nothing makes sense."

"Nothing ever makes sense."

"Then tell me now."

"Please, Lisa, you are taxing me." That meant question time was over. Obstinate, I held firm. "One more question."

Mama's look of defeat grew.

"Did Daddy cry when his daughter died?"

Mama scratched her face. She ran the back of her hand across her nose and then she picked at loose threads in my white bedspread. I was about to ask the question again when she said, "You love your little dog, Dino Martin, don't you?"

"Yes'um. I sure do." I couldn't help but love that dog. Dino was all about joy. He thumped his tail like a drummer, dug in the dirt with an unknown mission, and whenever I came outside, he wagged his butt to his head overjoyed to see me.

"When he dies, you'll have a bit of an idea of what it's like for a parent to lose a child." Then Mama was all cheery again. She kissed my forehead. "Sleep tight, don't let the bed bugs bite."

She turned off the light and pecan footballs etched my ceiling. I did not want my dog to ever die, until then, the thought of his demise had never occurred to me. My heart just about flew out of my throat. I thought again of the men in their pig-nosed mask on the muddy battlefield. I saw squatty little Dino loping through the mud, scared, whimpering. I pulled the covers over my head.

The next day, before it got dark and while the lightning bugs still flitted across the front yard, I found Daddy sitting on the front porch swing drinking a highball out of a pink plastic Tupperware glass. He stared out at the road. Grandma and Grandpa had gone to Shoney's Big Boy for dinner. It was their once-a-month night out.

"I know about your other wife and kid," I said, standing next to him.

"Ugh."

"I'm sorry you lost your daughter."

"Um."

"It probably hurt a lot, her being your first child. You must have loved her something awful."

He jiggled the ice in his highball and looked up at the pecan trees in the front yard, as if the words he was looking for were hanging on a high branch.

"Remember that story I never finished telling you?"

I nodded.

"Your grandfather had said to me that day, after we started hitting each other, I wouldn't make a good father to my unborn child, meaning Ava. I had all but lost contact with my first daughter, and then she passed on. But it wasn't like that. I tried to keep in touch. Life just gets in the way."

"What do you mean?" A knot formed in my stomach. His expression was changing, his lips drawing into themselves, his wrinkles deepening. I understood somehow that life as I knew it would be different from here on out. Daddy and I were walking together into undiscovered territory. I needed him to be my guide, yet I could not count on him.

"Things happen. You get busy, you get preoccupied, so preoccupied you're exhausted. You'll know what I mean when you are older. That's the end of the story."

He took a large sip of his drink and his face went back to normal; he continued staring high into the tree, seeing something no one else could. We sat there in silence for a long time. The sun started to go down and the lightening bugs came out, flitting around the yard like tiny lit-up souls.

"You want me to teach you how to throw a football, Doodie?" he asked me after a long time.

"Okay." We didn't have a football. Maybe he'd take me downtown on Saturday and we would pick one out, like a father and son would do. I wanted to be a little boy for Daddy, because I knew little girls were bad luck. They either died or dated white trash like Lewis Mitchum. I was the last hope. I had to be good. I had to stay alive and not pick a bad man.

I felt bad for wanting to leave my family, for wanting to get out of Newitville. But I saw where I got it, from my own parents. Two people trying to make the best out of life and just screwing it up routinely.

"Hold on." Daddy went inside the house and came out a few minutes later with a football. I had no idea where he got it. Daddy was Santa Claus, Harry Houdini, and God all under one skin.

He pointed to the azalea bushes framing the edge of our front lawn. "Go long," he said. I took off running backwards like I had seen the Ole Miss rebels do. He cocked his arm back and the football zipped through the air, it looked brown and lovely and full of hope. I held my arms straight up with my palms raised. The ball landed right in my hand. I cradled it to my chest.

Chapter Three
Gnarled Branch Road

The roads in our county had names that evoked beauty: Sunny Meadow, Piney Knoll, Oak Valley, Mossy Brook. Our road was the exception. We lived on Gnarled Branch, which could sum up our part of the family.

My father's side of the family lived in South Carolina in beach houses. Their back yards were the Atlantic Ocean. They frolicked in the waves and had clambakes. My mother's relatives lived in New Orleans and had large noisy family gatherings at weekends and worked in family-oriented law firms and banks where no one worked long hours because they couldn't wait to get home to their happy spouses and children.

Our family unit — my parents, me, Ava, Grandma and Grandpa — were in the minority of our blood relations. Of course Pie and Teckla and their kids also lived in Newitville, but that was that of the relatives. We were the small, Mississippi branch.

All our relatives lived in nice houses, even Pie and Teckla. Our house had two main rooms: the kitchen and living room. All other rooms fed off from them like petals on a deformed daisy. We had large rats in our attic and floors that creaked with the weight of our feet. Our walls were so thin you could hear a person whispering on the other side of the house and the tin roof had a layer of rust. There were dishpan-sized water spots on the living room ceiling, and during a good rain we had to keep buckets on the floor. Then there was the pecan tree outside my bedroom window, with its gnarled branch full of pecans that etched shadows on my ceiling and walls at night.

The Mississippi relations had one thing in common that made us different from the rest of the relatives: we had all the drunks. So much so that the other relatives speculated that living in Mississippi drove people to drink.

Grandpa had gone cold turkey years before I was born when he took my sister Ava, then four, for a "drive" in his Studebaker. She had been crying uncontrollably over some kid thing, like a broken toy or having to eat Brussels Sprouts. The drive ended about a mile down the road out on Highway 61 at a dive called the Wagon Wheel, a bar famous for the decayed wagon wheel planted out front in the gravel parking lot. Grandpa thought she would like a cola. And he knew he'd like a little Jim Beam.

He came home drunk a few hours later. Grandma stood at the kitchen door waiting for him, her arms hidden behind her back. Grandpa held Ava, who sucked her thumb; her eyes glazed from the nips of Jim Beam Grandpa had given her.

Grandma told him to put Ava to bed, which he did. When he returned to the kitchen, she calmly said, "You know something you damned sonofabitch? You just took your last Goddamned drink."

She had been hiding a cast iron skillet behind her back. With one swift move, she thrust it forward and rapped him up side the head — but not so hard that it would kill him. Just enough to knock him senseless, or to knock senses into him depending on the perspective. Grandpa fell to the ground and Grandma said, "Have I cured you yet?"

"What the hell are you doing?"

"Are you cured of the drink yet?"

"You'd have to hit me harder than that."

So she did.

That's when Grandpa gave up the bottle. This woman made drinking hurt too much.

Perhaps it was the fact that the patriarch stopped and the children did not that made Grandma so relentless in her pursuit to shame Mama and my aunts into stopping. She would cry (though her eyes were dry) as she whimpered to them, "I don't know why God has punished me so. I've never took a drop of liquor in my life and yet He's given me children who suck the bottle like it's milk."

This tactic wore Teckla down by the time I was eleven. My aunt was soon the leader of the local AA. She spent her morning calling the other members to check on their sobriety, chain smoking the whole time with a steaming cup of strong black coffee sitting in front of her at the kitchen table.

Pie continued drinking privately. My parents knew however, because every time Pie came over, their liquor supply mysteriously decreased an inch or two. They never told Grandma, but they would talk about it in front of me. It became something of our family secret.

Mama and Daddy were resilient to Grandma's preaching. Grandma generally left Daddy alone since he wasn't her child; she felt it was not her place. But with Mama she put a full-throttle effort into making her give up booze. Sometimes, while my wobbly mother washed the dinner dishes, Grandma would throw up her hands and scream in the middle of the kitchen, "Why God, why have you forsaken me?" Then she'd throw in a line about her ungrateful alcoholic children and my mother would stop wobbling and give a blue-jay screech, "I'M NOT UNGRATEFUL AND I'M NOT AN ALCOHOLIC."

Then Mama would cry and Grandma would start crying for real. Grandpa would hide in his bedroom watching television while Daddy screamed at Mama and Grandma from in front of the TV, "FOR GOD'S SAKE PLEASE SHUT YOUR GOD-DAMNED MOUTHS!"

On my twelfth birthday, Daddy gave me a gift of sorts. He called me into the bathroom where he and my mother were having their happy hour, safe from Grandma's Godly eyes. Sinatra played on their old portable record player. "Fly me to the moon," he crooned. Daddy sat on the toilet with the lid down, drinking a highball and tapping his left foot out of rhythm with the music. It took him a few moments to notice I had walked in.

"There you are! Doodie, we're moving." He jiggled the ice in his highball.

Before I could decide how I felt, he began describing the new home. "It's a place out on old Highway 80. I bet you've noticed it. It sits back from the road, and it has a huge lawn. I'll need to get a riding mower just to keep the grass cut; it's too much of a job to do it with a push mower. The house is practically a mansion."

"It is?" He had my full focus.

Daddy nodded, proud, pleased. "It's got five bedrooms, an upstairs and a downstairs and . . ." he waited, I could almost hear a drum roll, his pause had such momentous proportions, "it's got a swimming pool in the back yard!"

The pool cinched it for me, even though I intuitively understood this move meant Grandma and Grandpa were staying behind. As much as I loved them, they loved me more, like no one loved me. They told me daily I was their queenie, I was their cream cake, I was their puff of delight. I knew this move would be good though, that my parents and I should move before someone killed someone or one of them got carted off to the mental hospital over in Jackson.

Ava didn't pose an issue. She lived across the river in Monroe, with Lewis Mitchum, who she had finally married. She would barely notice if we never called her again, much less moved away. So the only downside was leaving my grandparents.

"Can we afford this new place?" I asked Daddy, suspecting that maybe he'd had too much Jack Daniel's and this was no more than a harebrained idea.

"Some old lady lives there, her name is Cain. She's a little crazy if you ask me, but she said her kids are worthless and she doesn't want them to sell the house and get the money after she's gone, so she's selling it to me for only $25,000. Doodie, I think we can swing it. I talked to Joe Poindexter down at the bank today. He says it looks good."

"I think her kids are going to step in and screw this up for us," Mama said. She took a swill of drink and wiped her lips. "They are some damn greedy bastards. I know the daughter. Selma Wyatt. She's very country club, you know. I see her in the grocery store sometimes wearing a tennis outfit. I think she's just showing off."

"Ah no, hell, Belle, you always have to be negative, don't you? It's old lady Cain's house, if she wants to sell it, Selma Wyatt can't stop her."

"Where is Mrs. Cain going to live?" I needed the facts. I could feel a swell of something quivering and expanding in my gut, a red-hot exclamation point, unfurling; it wiggled with growing life.

"She's going over to that new retirement village outside Bovina. She wants to be around people her own age." He pointed a finger at Mama, "And I tell you, she said, 'Tingle, I'm tired of my damned grandkids coming over here every afternoon to swim. They make too much damn noise.'"

"It's not going to happen."

I looked at Mama, not really seeing her through the image I had in my head of that beautiful large house, with its expansive yard and pool, an oasis hidden in the backyard.

"Na-uh," she said. "Na-uh."

For the next two weeks, Daddy came home with nightly updates on the move. "I had a talk with the bank today. We can swing this deal, but I'm going to owe them the rest of my life. Hell, Doodie, you may be paying the note on this house after I'm gone!"

On a Friday afternoon he came home and said, "Old lady Cain showed me around this afternoon. The house is perfect. There ain't a crack anywhere. And clean! Boy she keeps it so clean you could eat off the floors."

Then he said, "She wants us to come over tomorrow. Doodie, she said to bring your swimsuit!"

Even Mama was starting to get the faith.

"Imagine having your own pool!" She shivered with the thought and took a sip of her highball to calm herself.

I could not sleep that night. I lay in bed and marveled at how special my life was about to become. The timing of everything happening near my birthday made me feel like the center of the universe. There was a God, and he had an eye just on me. My parents, my grandparents — even my sister — all had lived their adult lives trying to make ends meet, never having enough, always wanting more. Here I was, barely twelve, and I would soon live in a fabulous house with an even more fabulous pool in the backyard. A quivering red-hot exclamation mark in my stomach started to grow.

Mirabella Cain had been a great beauty. I know, because this is one of the first things she said after being introduced. "Come here and look at my picture gallery." She took my hand and led me into her study. We left my parents standing in the foyer gazing at her collection of ceramic owls that framed the wall. In her study were old photographs of Mirabella in her youth, all colorized. She had Veronica Lake's hair and Greta Garbo's chin. That's what she told me, at least.

She lifted my own chin and looked at me. "You're a cutie pie, but you'll never be a looker on my level." She pointed a leathery finger to my head, then to my heart. "You better work on developing one of those two. A person needs beauty, brains, or heart to make them stand out."

"Yes'um."

"Did you bring your swimsuit?"

"Yes'um." I had it on underneath my little sundress. Mama had bought the suit for a Fourth of July swim party last summer at the Elks Lodge. It was a bikini; the top was a spangle of red, white, and blue stars, the bottom was three thick stripes in the same color. I could never swim in the ocean in that thing, for fear of attracting sharks. But for my future pool, it was perfect because everything was perfect.

Mirabella turned me around and gave me a swift spank on my bottom. "Okay then. The bathroom is the first door on your left in the hall."

I looked at her over my shoulder, uncertain as to why she told me this.

"Go. Go change," she said, impatient.

I had intended to just peel off my dress and flop into the pool, but this was still Mrs. Cain's house, and if she wanted me to change in the bathroom, then that's what I'd do.

The bathroom looked like something that might belong to a movie star. It wasn't quite pink or peach, but something soft and muted, yet bright and shiny. It conjured up a dreamy designer color, like dusky rose. The vanity mirror had Hollywood dressing room light bulbs in a row across the top. There were cherubs engraved in the sink bowl.

I touched the porcelain carefully, wanting to feel the realness of its beauty. It was cold and clean. In our home, Grandma and Grandpa's bathroom only had a toilet, claw-footed tub and a bare light bulb hanging from the ceiling on a frayed wire. My parents' bathroom was a little nicer as they had remodeled it. Daddy had asked himself what Frank Sinatra's bathroom would look like, if Frank were on a budget.

I got down on my knees in Mrs. Cain's bathroom and prayed, pressing my palms together. I felt silly; I was not religious. Mama had been a Catholic, Daddy a Methodist. To compromise, they both became Episcopalian. But they weren't that dedicated to their new faith and Grandma said if they didn't take me to church more, I'd end up a heathen.

But I wanted something big, so I felt like I had to call on the Almighty if he existed and was listening.

"Dear God, please, please, please let us get this house. I know we don't deserve it. It is too beautiful for the likes of people like us who eat off TV trays and keep plastic flowers in milk bottle vases, but if you let us have this house I swear as you are my witness I will never sin. I will not cuss, I will not lie, and I will never drink or murder anyone or kiss a boy until it's time for me to get married. I will make straight A's and I'll keep this beautiful house clean."

Then I took off my sundress and stripped down to my star-spangled bikini. I folded the dress over twice then shoved it under my arms along with my white plastic daisy sandals. I checked my reflection in the mirror; it would soon be my mirror. We would live in a house with cherubs in the bathroom.

I handed my bundle to Mama, who stood next to Daddy in the study; both commenting to Mrs. Cain that yes, she had been a beautiful young lady and how lucky she was to have grown into such an elegant mature matron.

"I'm ready," I said, standing there in my swimsuit.

Mirabella looked at me and frowned. "Young lady, consider propriety please."

I glanced around the room. "Yes ma'am, you've got nice property," I said.

"I'm talking about properness, not property, child. Doesn't she have a cover-up?" She looked at my mother. My mother reached inside the Jitney Jungle paper sack she had brought along as a beach bag, and pulled out a red and yellow bath towel with fat alternating stripes.

"Cover up, Doodie." She handed it to me. I wrapped it around my body and looked at Mirabella, who sighed and pointed. "The pool is through that door."

I stood at the edge and looked down into the blue. I had observed from staring enviously at many a pool, whether it belonged to a motel or one of my parents' friends, that there were two types of pool water: aqua Marine water or deep blue. Mirabella Cain had a pool that went beyond the latter. It was the color of stars in the velvet night sky. I stuck my toe in and felt warmth. I took a deep breath and dived. My body slid through satin, and made a swooshing sound as I pierced the surface with a swelling gurgle of pressure against my ears. I popped to the top and rubbed the starriness off of my face. The sun hit the water, reflecting gold daggers. I treaded, taking in everything: the chlorine: the smell of the freshly cut large backyard, the sound of the neighbor's dog barking a quarter mile down the road, the thudded roar of cars on Old Highway 80 at the edge of the long driveway.

We would live here soon, I could believe it now. This would be mine. We would still live on a road with an ugly name in a county of roads with names of beauty, but we would live in a large house with cherubs in the bathroom and a pool, blue as a star, in the backyard. I put a hand to my stomach feeling that exclamation point in my body as it cooled from red-hot to gold.

Grandma was not pleased to hear we were moving. She told Mama, "I don't know if we can make it on our own. All we get is our social security check and Daddy's VA."

Mama said, "The note on this place isn't that much. And with it just being you two, the light bill won't be so bad. You never eat out. Honest, Mama, other than those two things, you don't spend any money." Mama started to cry. "We want to do this for Lisa. You should have seen her face when she was in that pool. She's never lit up like that."

"It's him, isn't it?"

"Rodney? It's me too. Hell, we want a nice house. We want our own place. Mama, we're drowning here. We can't go on like this. You and Daddy hate Rodney and we can't have anything of our own."

Grandma raised her voice, saying we already had everything of our own. Mama started in about all her sacrifices for this family and Grandma said, "Oh there you go again."

I closed my bedroom door and turned up my radio. At night, we could pick up a Chicago AM station. I liked to turn off the lights and imagine myself as some Yankee child, living up there in the big, blustery city. I imagined Chicago as a fat millionaire with shoulder pads: large, tough, substantial. It was the nearest Northern city, and I had many dreams about growing up and running away there. I would become a famous writer and eat lobster over a candlelight dinner in my penthouse, looking out over the lights of the city, a view laden with golden stars. It's not that Chicago itself was so appealing, but the idea of living in a big city, plus I had wanted a penthouse since I could remember. Or any nice house, one without pack rats in the attic, rust on the roof, and water spots on the ceiling.

All of my friends lived in nice homes with carpets and dimmer light switches and insulation in the attic and walls thick enough that you could tell secrets safely. I never brought my friends home, afraid that after seeing our place, they would talk about me behind my back, that everyone in school would soon know about the leaky roof or the pack rats playing their scratchy symphony over our heads.

Mrs. Cain's house wasn't a Chicago penthouse, it was better because it was in Newitville where I would be the envy of the town. But now Grandma was trying to stop us.

I believed she didn't want us to go because she loved me too much. I was the youngest, and in my family, the most revered. I was small and said stupid yet amusing things that made the adults laugh. I had the blessing and the curse of the disgustingly cute.

I had to make her love me less so she wouldn't fight the move, because my mother and father could not win against her. She had a tongue and a mind sharper than the claws of the pack rat in the attic.

That night, I listened to the constant scratching of the rats. Their claws played the wood and asbestos like symphonic instruments. I always wanted to get a flashlight and crawl up there, with Grandma by my side, wielding her garden hoe. She would kill any rat that got too close to me. But I wanted to see what the creatures were doing that they made so much noise, and why they were active only after the sun went down. Daddy, in an ineffective effort to calm me, said they were vampire rats and were nocturnal. I didn't have to worry about them sucking my blood, they were more interested in snakes. That's why the adults didn't try too hard to kill them. Grandpa had put traps up there, but the rats were too smart. And they were large. Grandma said they were the size of beagles. I started picturing spotted beagles in the attic.

I worried about the safety of Snoopy, our cat. He lived on the tin roof of our house. Snoopy was afraid of the yard dogs. We now had four: Frank Sinatra, Sammy Davis Jr., Peter Lawford and, of course, Dino Martin. Daddy called them the rat pack in a hopeful attempt to emulate his hero, Sinatra. Everyday at 5:00, Snoopy would show up on the roof over the back door. He balanced on the rain gutter and yowled till someone climbed a ladder and fed him. I feared a beagle-rat would get out of the attic and eat him.

But this particular night, I didn't think too much about the beagle-rats or my cat. I lay in bed and wondered what I could do to make Grandma love me less. She always said Daddy was lazy and watched too much television. And, of course, she hated the drinking.

So I decided I had to get drunk and sit on my ass and watch television.

The next morning, after my parents left for work, I went into their bathroom. Mama kept a small dish rack next to the sink to dry their bar utensils and highball glasses. I took Daddy's Ole Miss Tumbler, which had a Colonel Reb emblem on the front, and filled it halfway with Jack Daniel's, then I went into the kitchen, plopped in some ice cubes and topped it off with Coca-Cola. I drank it down, making a face, wondering how my parents could drink three or four times a night. I think it was then that I understood what Grandma was yammering about when she said they had a problem. That was the only explanation for drinking.

I forced myself to have another. Then I threw up.

Grandma heard me and rushed into the bathroom. "Why are you sick?"

"I drank Jack Daniel's."

"Why the hell did you do that?"

I couldn't answer, because I started heaving again. She wet a washcloth and held it against my throat.

When I finished, she asked, "Are you better?" Her face, always mapped with age, now looked like a series of canyons, evidence of her concern.

"Yes."

She told me to continue holding the cloth. Then she went outside, got a switch, came in and told me to bend over.

"No. You aren't my mother," I said. I folded my arms across my chest and stared at her with eyes she saw whenever she looked in the mirror.

"I cook your dinner, I sew your clothes, I worry about you when you're sick. I may not be your mother, but I was sure as hell given the job. Bend your ass over."

"No."

Grandma was a round woman, short as me. She wore her hair in a bun and despite her weight and her leathery skin, her hair always looked perfect. At this moment, stray strands fell around her sweaty neck. Her body jiggled like Jell-O she was so mad. Then she started to do something I hadn't counted on: cry. My parent's drinking made her cry, but not me, not her puff of delight. I never even imagined I could drive her to tears. I had simply wanted to make her love me less, and had not considered the possible consequences.

"Goddamn you," she cried. "Goddamn you and your mother and your Goddamned father. I do and do for you people and I tried to protect you from their ways and this is the thanks I get. You're drinking and they want to move out. Well move out. I don't give a Goddamn anymore. You can all rot in hell, you ungrateful little bastards!"

She let the switch drop and walked through the kitchen to her bedroom and, honest, the sound she made the entire time could only be described as deep, full-throttle boo-hooing.

It was the quietest summer day I ever spent. I had to go back to bed, the Jack Daniel's had made me so sick. Grandma stayed in her room for a couple of hours, then she went out to her garden and worked there till four, hoeing, hoeing, hoeing, God only knows what she was hoeing. Grandpa was beside himself with worry. He kept going outside and giving her water. I managed to go out once, for a few minutes. I spied on her from the middle of the corn rows and watched as the hateful sun beat down on her fat, wrinkled body. I had to be standing a good thirty yards away, and I swear I could smell her sweat. She kept mopping her neck and forehead with a handkerchief. And then she would raise her hoe high in the air and chop the ground. I know she was chopping at all the years of misery my little family had caused her, me, Mama and Daddy, and probably Ava, who made her miserable by moving away.

I had succeeded in making Grandma love me less, and it hadn't taken much. Just two drinks and some vomit. I thought, Life is easy. I thought, I'm the master of my destiny. I thought, I'm not as happy as I thought I would be.

I went back to bed, held my stomach and tried to console myself with thoughts of the swimming pool behind that grand house.

When Mama and Daddy came home that night, I went into the bathroom and told them what I had done because I knew Grandma would tell them as soon as she got a chance. Right then, though, she was soaking in a tub of ice water because Grandpa was sure she had sunstroke and he made it clear that if she did, it was my fault and my Goddamned parents' fault for upsetting her so.

Mama and Daddy were shocked that I had been drinking.

"Why? You drink," I said.

"We're adults, that's different," Daddy said.

I explained why I had done this: so that Grandma would get mad at me and not fight us on moving. "I did it for you two, really," I said, summing up my sacrifice.

Mama softened and Daddy looked away. "Oh Doodie," she said. "Tell her Rodney."

Daddy pulled me on his lap.

"We aren't moving, Doodie."

He might as well have said, "The aliens have landed and taken over." His words were unreal, like something from a nightmare.

"Pumpkin, old lady Cain is crazy. She says she never told me she would sell me that house. She has totally gone back on her word. Hell, she downright lied."

"That crazy old coot even went as far as saying that she would never even think of selling a house to us because we had no propriety," Mama said.

"What?" My stomach punched my rib cage. I think a bit of the Jack Daniel's had hid at the bottom of my belly and now it was ready to come out.

"She told your daddy that she would never even think of selling to us because you came to her house and didn't have a proper bathing suit cover-up."

I squirmed off Daddy's lap. "Then it's my fault."

"Hell no, the bitch is crazy!" Daddy said.

My face went hot, my muscles coiled. The golden exclamation mark that had lived inside me since the beginning of this whole thing, had been slowly withering all day, and had now officially died. It shrunk into a small black period.

"Honey, Doodie, this is not your fault."

"Okay."

I went to bed. It was only six o'clock. I stared out the window, past the gauzy curtains Grandma took out of the closet and hung every summer so my room could have more light, and so I could lay in bed and look at the old tree out the window. She had said to me once that the tree was special, because it had to be three hundred years old or something like that. "Think of all the things it's seen, Lisa. That tree is older than me." I had never heard her voice so tinkly and youthful as that day. I never thought of my grandmother as young, because she had always been old since I knew her. But she told me that as a little girl she climbed trees. She liked the name of the road we lived on because it reminded her of the trees she used to climb down in the backwater country of Lake Pontchartrain in Southern Louisiana. Gnarled Branch. "A gnarled branch is the best. They can hold your weight because they're so strong."

The tree outside my window had nothing but gnarled branches, but they were too high for me to climb. I stared at it until the light faded and the beagle-rats began scratching above in the attic.

After a while, Grandma came into my room with a malted milkshake.

"Drink this," she said, sitting on my bed. I could tell she was no longer mad at me.

"Your mother told me what that was all about this morning."

"Yes ma'am."

"Are you sorry?"

"I sure am."

"Lisa, we judge ourselves by our intentions, and we judge other people by the way they live their lives. That's why the world is ruined."

"Yes ma'am."

I finished the malt, and she kissed my forehead. "Tomorrow you'll feel better after a good night's sleep."

She may have been right, but the beagle rats were very active, and I could not sleep. Snoopy crawled over the tin roof; I could hear it pop under his paws. I got up around midnight, grabbed a flashlight, and went into the yard. Peter Lawford, Frank Sinatra, Sammy Davis, Jr. and Dino Martin all wagged their tails at me, their sleepy eyes smiling. Dino Martin, who loved me more than the others did, whined a little wanting me to pet him. The four of them slept on the side porch, which was exposed to the yard without a screen. They curled up around each other, full of love and ticks. My poor father. The only rat pack this family had was that pack of beagle-rats in the attic.

Snoopy yowled when I moved the ladder from where we normally fed him. I placed it next to the attic grate. He plodded over the tin, which made small thunder noises under his weight. He meowed as I reached the top rung.

I cooed at him for a moment, then I peered the flashlight in through the lattice and shone it into the dark attic. There was a thudding scurry. I followed the sound, catching a glimpse of something large and dark and a flash of red eyes. I saw another quick movement, just out of the beam's ray and I moved the light, landing it on a large, heaving rat. Its claws were as long as its teeth and I almost fell back, frightened. I grabbed on to the side of the ladder and steadied myself and when I looked again, the rat was gone.

I climbed down and went back to the dogs. Snoopy followed alongside, on the roof. After seeing those rats, I knew "beagle" was not an adequate description. Bobcat was more like it. I lay down with the dogs and above I could hear Snoopy settling onto the tin. It occurred to me then that during the day he must have gone somewhere cooler, else the tin would get too hot for his paws. The only possibility was the old tree outside my window. He must have crawled up the trunk and into the branches. He probably rested there all day. That same tree was probably how the rats got in the attic. One tree carried a creature I loved, as well as creatures I feared and, meanwhile, it never stopped being beautiful and sturdy. Old lady Cains' house may have been more luxurious, but it didn't have a tree like the one outside my window at home, and it wouldn't have been home without Grandma and Grandpa, even without all the fighting. It would have seemed bare and lonely.

I put my head on Dino Martin's belly, finally ready to sleep. I did not worry about the ticks or fleas that might get in my hair. I knew tomorrow Grandma would pick them out.

Chapter Four
A Used Woman

In 1975 my sister Ava got self-esteem. She read a self-help book called *I'm Okay, You're Okay*. Evidently her latest husband Herbie was not okay. Ava left him like she left Lewis before him, citing "irreconcilable differences," as her reason. "I say he's a jackass and he doesn't agree," she told us.

As part of her freedom, she decided to begin a year long training program for the Ms. Divorced Mississippi pageant. She had long harbored a desire to be a professional beauty and make money on her looks. Ava had good hair: thick with strength, brown with luster, shoulder length with an ardent flip. The girl could coif like no one else. Her skin didn't know what it meant to go without moisturizer. Unfortunately, at just five foot five, she didn't have a model's stature, though she was super thin, which meant she had won half the battle in the modeling world. She had strange diet habits: she would only eat Grandma's peach cobbler. One day—not too far in the future— there would be a household word for women like my sister. Anorexic. Back then in Newitville they just figured she was malnourished.

She had been hospitalized a few years earlier. My parents, believing they were sheltering me, told me she had gone to stay at the beach with my grandmother in South Carolina. I asked why I couldn't go and they said, "Because Ava is Grandma Lizbeth's special girl."

I started to cry. To make me feel better; Mama said that I was the apple of Great Aunt Maxine's eye. Aunt Maxine wore black dresses with nurse's shoes dyed black. She spoke Cajun French much of the time, knowing full well that most of the relatives couldn't understand a word she was saying. One of my earliest memories is of her trying to force me to switch from using my left hand. She told my mother, in front of me (and in a rare moment of English), that growing up left-handed could ruin me, as southpaws were notoriously bad with math.

"She won't be able to handle money," she screamed. "The best she can hope for in a job is as a movie usher."

So when I heard that Aunt Maxine loved me best, I cried harder, feeling that I only appealed to really mean people. I wanted to be loved by sweet old ladies like Grandma Lizbeth, who smelled of Noxzema and baked gingerbread cookies in the middle of July for no other reason than they evoked Christmas.

Shortly after Ava left Herbie, she discovered she was pregnant. The thought of being a single mother, or worse, going back to Herbie, must have sent her into shock. She lost the baby, and this time my parents really did ship her off to Grandma Lizbeth's to recuperate. They never told me she had lost the baby — I found out years later. The thing is, I had known that Ava was pregnant as the day she found out, she came home from the doctor's screaming that she was carrying that "worthless bastard's child!" Mama rushed her into the bathroom so they could whisper-scream at each other and work out a plan for "what to do now."

Ava didn't return from Grandma Lizbeth's until after the divorce was finalized, many months later. It took so long that I thought she had given birth. When Ava came back, thin as ever and wearing a tight dress, I looked at her tiny waist and wondered how she managed to get so skinny so quick. She even sported a new flip-do, which looked like it required fuss. Most new mothers I had seen had cut off their hair just to cope with the new burden of child rearing.

"You don't look like you've had a baby," I said.

Ava said, "Why would I look like that?"

"Because you did."

She realized that I didn't know about the miscarriage, and that made it all seem fresh again. She started to cry. Mama took me aside and in what had to be the biggest lie she ever told me or anyone, she said, "Ava had the baby while she was in South Carolina. She had to give it up for adoption since she's divorced now." Then she warned me, "Never bring this up with anyone, you hear. This is private family stuff."

I should have known something was amiss right there. Mama had no compunction whatsoever about sharing personal family matters with total strangers. On the day I got my period, she took me to Jitney Jungle to buy Kotex and told everyone in line, "My daughter just started menstruating!"

For a few years, I actually thought I had a niece or nephew running around South Carolina. I developed feelings for the child, thinking I would have been a wonderful aunt. I had every intention of one day hiring a detective to hunt the kid down. I had fantasies of walking up to her door (I just knew Ava had had a daughter) and looking into the face of someone who resembled me and saying, "Hey, I'm your aunt. Let's go get a burger and catch up." I'd give her fashion advice and help her strategize her career. She was going to be a famous journalist, just like her Aunt Lisa. I didn't find out the truth till college, when I came home one weekend. I called for Judy, my rat terrier dog.

Daddy said, "Doodie, Judy died a month ago. We didn't tell you because we wanted some time to pass, so it would be easier on you." Of course, that made no sense. In the height of my grief, I brought up my niece, saying I wanted to find her, and they looked at me like I had fallen off the turnip wagon. I spent a week in bed, grieving the loss of both Judy and Bonnie, the name I had given my niece.

When Ava returned from South Carolina after the divorce, we all focused on getting her ready for the Mrs. Divorced Mississippi Pageant. My mother, in particular, supported this goal and rallied my father, Grandma, and Grandpa.

I could never quite get on board. It just involved too much drama, a condition that seemed perpetual to Ava. We had never been close and were as opposite as two ends of a row. We went through our lives at different stages. When I was still playing with Ken and Barbie, she was actually dressing like Barbie, running loose around Newitville man-hunting for a Ken type. My first love had been Davy Jones of the Monkees; hers had been Paul McCartney. I later loved Donny Osmond, she liked Cat Stevens. I dug in the dirt with my dogs, she took baths.

Things changed when I turned fourteen; that was the same year as the pageant. I began to view my big sister as an asset — sometimes. She knew about makeup, and she certainly knew about guys. I had visions of the two of us hanging out at the mall, having lunch and confiding to each other about our love interests.

But Ava did not want love that year. She wanted retribution. Grandma Lizbeth, a fallen debutante (her wealthy family had lost every penny during the Depression and her husband, my daddy's daddy, had run off to San Diego and shacked up with a woman from Mexico), drilled it into Ava's head that the best revenge was happiness. She asked Ava what would make her happy, and Ava said, "To be Miss Mississippi."

As this could not happen because of the divorce, Lizbeth suggested the idea of Ms. Divorced Mississippi. She told Ava, "Sugar, when life gives you lemons, make some goddamn lemonade."

Ava agreed with her entire heart, soul and vanity. So our family dove headfirst into helping Ava realize her dream.

Everyone did it for different reasons. My mother felt bad for her oldest daughter, believing that Ava's life had been ruined by the divorce and she wasn't that far into her twenties. "She's spoiled goods," is how she put it.

Daddy was less subtle. One night at dinner, he said, "Damn, you are going to have one hell of a hard time finding a man. No fellow likes a used woman." Then he said, "You know, if you win this damn thing, some doctor might just marry you. I mean, you'll be a status symbol, sort of."

Grandma, Mama's mama, helped Ava out of love. She knew Ava really wanted and needed this pageant, and if it made her happy, then Grandma Emily would do whatever it took to help. Even if that meant forcing Grandpa to help, which he reluctantly did. Grandpa was not a people person. He never said much, and helping Ava meant potentially interacting with the whole family including Daddy.

As for me, I was just the kid. I did what I was told.

Ava went on an orange diet, which meant she ate orange food only. She had a real fondness for sweets, and she reasoned that as long as she ate only one kind of food, she would be thin. That limited her diet to orange Jell-O and pumpkin pie. The sugar seemed to fortify her. And Daddy's little jibe about her being used goods didn't rattle her at all.

"Don't worry about me none, Daddy cakes," she had told him. "As soon as I wrap that Mrs. Divorced Mississippi banner around my torso, I'll have cute doctors and lawyers fawning all over me. I might be used goods, but I'll have a tiara."

The pageant stands out in the Tingles' family history because it is the only time that we were all behind a cause: get Ava that crown. We each had a job. Grandma sewed her gown. Daddy talked her up to Lewis Hornsby, Mrs. Edna Crowler, and Charles Nick, all pageant judges in the contest. Mama worked with Ava on her talent, the monologue from *Gone with the Wind* where Scarlet swears she will never starve again (the irony was not lost on me, as my sister only ate orange food).

Grandpa's job was to drive slowly behind Ava in his car as she jogged – the purpose never being clear. This was Mama's idea and I think she just liked the way it looked, like Ava was important — a perception building tactic on my mother's part, just in case any judges happened by. Grandpa said he did it for fear she might faint. He said she was so thin she had no business running.

My job was to brush her hair nightly, one hundred times and to apply her nightly facial of egg whites and honey. By the time the pageant rolled around, I had such an aversion to eggs and honey that I could not eat baked goods for a year.

The big day came and Ava sparkled. The night before, Grandma had given her hair an olive oil conditioner, so her hair looked glossy. That morning, Ava brushed her teeth for five minutes with baking soda, and rubbed Vaseline over them so it would be hard not to smile. She wore Chanel #5 and three-inch heels.

She and I spent the afternoon at Fanny's Beauty Mart, where my aunts, Pie and Teckla, were also getting their hair done. While Fanny poofed Ava's hair, I made sure all my sister's needs were met, meaning, if she wanted some diet soda or water or anything, I got it for her. She kept sending me next door to the Jitney Jungle. First it was for a Tab. As soon as I got that, she sent me back for carrot sticks. I had to clean the carrots in the same sink Fanny used to dye women's hair, and the reek got into the vegetable.

"I feel like I'm eating red dye #8," Ava said, throwing a carrot at me. So I had to run over to the Western Sizzler salad bar and pick up a to-go carton of carrots. The cashier looked suspicious when I presented her with my purchase.

"Just carrots? You ain't one of those vegetarians, are you?" she asked me in a thick country drawl. She looked like the kind of stereotype Hollywood casting agents would pick for a movie about Mississippi: a fat bumpkin with teeth missing.

"No, the carrots are for my sister. She's a contestant in the Mrs. Divorced Mississippi Pageant."

"Oh, well, that explains it then."

I spent the rest of the afternoon listening to Fanny and my aunts giving Ava unremitting encouragement.

"Just throw your shoulders back and smile," Teckla told her. "When those judges see your pearly whites, they won't be able to help themselves."

"You've got the prettiest smile. It reminds me of the way my teeth used to look before I lost them," said Pie, sliding her false teeth out to show everyone. "These look pretty good, but sometimes they fall out right when I'm in the middle of a sentence."

"You should use DentaStix. It works for me," Teckla said. "Ava, you take care of your teeth, now, you hear, because your teeth are an asset."

"You haven't told your sister how pretty she looks," Fanny said. "Tonight's a big night for your sister. You ought to tell her what a beauty she is."

"You look good," I said.

"Children aren't much for words," Pie said and laughed like there was a joke everyone but me knew.

"I'm fourteen."

"Are you fourteen?" Teckla asked then turned to Ava before I could answer. "She's not developed much for fourteen. All the girls in the family were more developed by the time they were her age."

"She's a squirt," Pie said.

I looked at my breasts and then over at Ava, who was a good three or four bra sizes larger than me. I remembered seeing pictures of her when she was my age and she pretty much looked as she did now.

"I'm a thirty-two," I said, as if verifying my meagerness.

Pie tisked. Teckla looked sympathetic and Fanny cooed, "Don't you worry, baby, you'll grow some bazoombas one day."

"At least you've got your teeth," Pie said. "Course, you'll lose those one day."

Teckla pointed a finger to the side of her head. I thought she was imitating pulling a gun trigger. But then she said, "You've got you some brains. You'll use them to figure out how to get you a good man."

After the Beauty Mart, I didn't really feel up to a pageant. I had tiny breasts and sooner or later I'd lose my teeth. If I was lucky, I'd end up hanging out with a bunch of old women and rattle my false teeth around in my mouth. Ava was a nervous wreck driving over to the pageant, and she couldn't just ask me to do something, she had to grab my arm and claw me with her Opera Red nails.

"Listen, don't be a brat, do as I tell you." She was driving and reached over the car seat and dug into my wrist.

"Ow!" I yanked away. "What did you tell me?"

"Listen to me, will you?"

"Okay. What do you want?"

"I want you to change the radio station."

We met Mama and Daddy in the parking lot of the Holiday Inn, the place where the pageant would be held.

"Your grandparents can't make it," Mama said, greeting us. "Grandma's gout is acting up. I think it's all the excitement."

Ava acted like she didn't hear or care what Mama was saying. Tonight wasn't about the relatives who couldn't be here. It was all about Ava, the future Mrs. Divorced Mississippi.

Mama had Ava's dress and swimsuit on hangers and wrapped in plastic. Daddy carried her shoes in a tote bag. He was dressed in a forest green leisure suit and kept tugging at his yellow tie. Mama said, "How do I look?" She wore a royal blue dress with a corsage over her heart.

"You look good," Ava said, not looking at her. "I'm late. Come on, Lisa."

She took her clothes and shoes from Mama and Daddy and shoved them in my arms. "Let's go!" she barked.

Finally, it was just about time for the pageant. The hotel had converted the Steamboat Room, usually reserved for conferences, into dressing rooms for the contestants. There were ten women in total. Three were from Newitville, counting Ava. I knew one of the other two girls' families. Ava's main rival, Scarlett Traina, had a little sister, Melanie.

We were in the same grade and hated each other. She hung out with the In-Crowd, and I was in the Fringe-Crowd, composed mainly of fallen members of the In-Crowd. We weren't unpopular, we had just messed up in some way, either with bad grades, or getting caught talking bad about one of the In-Crowd royalty, or the royalty had just tired of us.

I had been demoted after telling Tiffany Blunt that Melanie got fingered by Hank Hines, and that she was so cavernous that he actually lost his wrist watch. I did not make this up. Monica Priestly told me.

It didn't matter who started the rumor, I'm the one who got caught because that red-headed snitch with constant braids, Marcy Howell, overheard me and Tiffany talking in the cafeteria at lunch, and she told Melanie who told everyone I was a backstabbing liar. The very next day I'm eating lunch at the table of the Fringe Crowd. Tiffany, too, because of guilt by association.

Ironically, the Fringe-Crowd was larger than the In-Crowd by two or three people, and I often wondered why we weren't the popular ones since we were the majority.

I wandered into the Mighty River Room, where the pageant would be held. A refreshment table had been set up for the family members. Mama and Daddy sat in the front row not far from the punch bowl. Daddy held a Dixie Cup in his hand, the pink from the drink inside showing through the thin paper. Mama held up her cup as I sat next to her and said, "Want some Pageant Punch?"

"No ma'am. I want to go home. Ava is being mean to me."

"Oh now, she's just nervous. This is a big event."

"Hell, those are some good-looking divorced gals," Daddy said, wiping the pink off his upper lip. "Ava should be nervous. She's got some stiff competition."

"Hush, Rodney. That's your own daughter you're talking about."

"And I'm telling you, there's some fine gals in this show."

Mama leaned over to me, her big face jiggly from all the excitement. "Tell me, does your old mama look good today?"

"Yes ma'am."

"Do you think so?" She touched her hair. "Fanny did my hair this morning. She put a rinse in it to take out the gray."

"You look good."

"Do I look fat?"

My mother stood five foot two and weighed 180 pounds. Her chin fell into her neck, and pale, plump turkey leg-like arms poked through the sleeveless dress she wore,.

"You look like you've lost some weight," I said. By asking me the fat question, she had succeeded in making me feel more sorry for her than I did for myself.

"It's hard you know, because this pageant isn't just about the contestants." She looked around the room at all the highly coifed, high-heeled mothers of the contestants. "There's a pageant in here too."

"You look good, Mama."

"Now I tell you who's good-looking: That Scarlett Traina woman is good-looking," Daddy said.

"Daddy."

"Hush, Rodney."

I excused myself, knowing Ava needed me. She hadn't sunk her claws into flesh for five minutes, and was overdue. As I walked away I heard Mama in a teary voice say to Daddy, "You haven't told me I look good today."

"Oh, hell, you look fine. Quit asking."

When I returned to the Steamboat Room, Ava and Scarlett were screaming at each other. They stood inches from each other's noses, yelling. Then Scarlett grabbed Ava's hair and pulled a ringlet loose. Ava kicked Scarlett in the shin. Scarlett reached down and rubbed the pain, "Now I'm going to have a bruise, you piece of trailer trash."

"I have *never*. . . *ever*. . . lived in a trailer."

"Y'all hush," said Mrs. Biedenhorn, the pageant hostess. She inserted herself in between the two women.

"You slept with my husband," Ava said.

"I would not lower myself like that. Your husband had a crush on me. You rank little thing, you weirdo. Who do you think you are, being in this pageant? You aren't pretty. You're just okay. The only thing you have going for you is that you're thin!"

The look on Ava's face told me that Scarlett had just done more than wound my sister; she had taken something away from her. Maybe a delusion. Ava was attractive, but I really didn't think she was pageant material. I would never say that, because around our house, my parents and grandparents spent a lot of time talking about Ava and her looks in front of her because of her weight problem. It was as if she were a miracle in the rose garden, the largest and reddest bloom of all. My family believed in my sister's beauty and sometimes, I looked in the mirror and saw that we had the same bumpy nose, with the same mole in the crook, and the same dark heredity blue lines under our eyes as our mother and grandmother.

Mrs. Biedenhorn told Scarlett, "You have a mean streak in you, missy. Now you apologize."

"I'm just telling the truth."

"Well sometimes the truth isn't the polite thing to say." Mrs. Biedenhorn put her hand to her mouth, "Oh now, Ava, that came out wrong. You are pretty. You are very pretty."

Fanny walked up, holding a brush, a hair clip snapped over the top of her collar. She had been over at another booth helping another girl poof her hair. "Now listen, Scarlett," she said, "I did your hair and I did Ava's today and I'm telling you something, you are both beautiful. You two girls smile pretty and make-up. This is just pre-show jitters.

Scarlett, you've always been too damn competitive for your own good. That is just not becoming. You be pretty now, you hear."

Scarlett seemed to respond to Fanny's cooing. She softened and said, "Well, she started it."

"Oh, excuse me, but you started it by sleeping with my husband," Ava said.

"Oh na-uh. That piece of dirt came on to me."

They lunged at each other, and I ran out of the room, to get Daddy or a pageant official or some Vaseline, something to slide on their teeth so they couldn't talk, only smile.

Scarlett had a big bruise on her shin by the time the swimsuit competition started. A straight strand of hair lay flat on Ava's hair, noticeable in all the curls. My cousins, Delia and Carson, were sitting behind us. I heard Carson say, "What the Faulkner? Fanny sure botched Ava's hair."

Mama had been crying. She wouldn't tell me why, but Daddy said, "Oh hell, she's mad because she says she's fat. She ain't fat. She's pleasingly plump is what I told her. It's not good for her to be around all these good-looking women."

Then he had to go and say with a leering laugh, "But it sure is good for me."

The pageant did not go well. Ava forgot one of her lines when reciting the monologue from *Gone with the Wind*, the part where Scarlett O'Hara says, "I will never starve again."

Scarlett Traina simply broke into tears when she dropped her baton, and ran off stage. She got in her car, I'm told, and drove straight to Jackson — in her evening gown. There's a good story about her that night that surfaced around town. She had gone into the IHOP off I-55 and was crying into her pancakes when a handsome young man walked up to her and offered her a wadded Kleenex. They started talking; she told him her story. He turned out to be a gynecologist at the Mississippi Medical Center. They married not too long after and, seven months later, she gave birth to a baby girl.

From the moment the kid could take a step and say "Goo-Goo" Scarlett started planning her life: signing her up for tap dancing, ballet, piano, and voice lessons. She told Fanny, "You can't get them started too young for the beauty pageants."

Ava didn't win; that probably goes without saying. Carlotta Jones took the crown, becoming the first black Mrs. Divorced Mississippi. She and Ava had gone to high school together, where Carlotta became the first black Newitville County High valedictorian. Ava finished somewhere in the fourth quartile of students.

After the pageant, my family and I stood around the stage, and nodded and smiled while family friends came up and told Ava, "Good job," or "It's a shame, hon, it's a real shame." Teckla said, "Ava, the Lord works in mysterious ways," to which my mother said, "Don't we know it."

As a consolation, Ava wanted to go to the Dixie Spirit Bowling Alley and eat corn-dogs. They had the best in town.

"Hell, I'm hungry," she said. "I haven't eaten since 1971."

Daddy stayed behind to help Ava pack up her things. He said he'd drive her in her car and meet me and Mama there.

Mama and I got in my parents' big brown Cordova and Mama peeled out of the parking lot.

"Whoa! Where's the fire?" I said. "You must really want a corn-dog."

I thought it was funny, but Mama's face was red and her eyes had this kind of wounded-fire look she would get when she didn't know whether to shed tears or scream. We stopped for a red light and Mama put her head on the steering wheel and started to cry. The light changed and she kept crying. Cars honked. The light changed back to red, then to green, and more cars honked. Finally they just started to pull around and drive on. On about the fourth light change, I said, "Mama, I think we should go."

She pulled over into the parking lot of the bowling alley. The neon sign posted high over the front door read Dixie Spirit. It flashed pink, red, green and blue, and cast a pretty glow on us.

"You look pretty in the Dixie Spirit light, Mama."

She wiped her tears and laughed. "Dixie Spirit light. That's funny. When you are older, if you decide to be in a beauty pageant, comedy should be your talent."

"I don't think I'm going to be in a beauty pageant, Mama."

My mother put her hand under my chin and studied my face. "No, I guess you won't. You look like your old mother, except you are much thinner."

"We all want to be beautiful."

"You are beautiful," she said, and I wanted to say, "But you just said I look like you." But I didn't want to cause her to cry anymore.

"Youth is hard, you know that. They say it's wasted on the young, but it's really just plain hard. There's so much pressure to be perfect. Little goddesses. That's the expectation I think we put on ourselves," Mama said.

"I feel old," I said.

"That's probably my fault. Ava's losing is my fault, and it's your Daddy's, too."

"How do you see that?"

"Sugar, it's always the parents' fault."

We sat in the car for the longest time, not saying a word. People came in and out of the bowling alley; people Daddy would call "skanky." Girls in tube tops, men with muscle shirts, overweight women wearing halter tops and overweight men wearing jeans too tight.

I saw a man touch his hand to his toupee before he went inside; a woman checked her reflection in the side mirror of a pick up truck. She gritted her teeth and used her fingernail as a toothpick. A young couple came out, her arms locked around his, her head on his shoulder and she giggled as he did a pig call. "*SUUUUEEEE!*"

I could tell that right then, at that time, she felt pretty, even though she and that guy might be the only people who thought that.

Daddy and Ava finally showed up. We got out and met them. Ava took one look at Mama and asked, "You okay?"

"I'm just tired. I could lay my bones down and die. Are you okay?"

'I'm fine. I don't know what I was thinking, to be honest. I'm just glad it's over."

Inside the bowling alley, balls struck pins and here and there, someone whooped while another hooted and there was general laughter. We ate, not saying much.

Ava ordered two corn-dogs and covered them both in mustard. She ate the first one in what seemed like a gulp. We watched, amazed she had an appetite. Mama smiled, and got teary eyed.

"Baby, you don't have any idea how good it is to see you eat. We worry about you so much."

"I know. I've ruined my life. I'm a loser. I'm a divorced loser. I married a cheater and, well, I'm a loser."

"You are not a loser," Mama said.

"Aw hell," Daddy said.

"You left your husband. That takes guts. You're brave," I said. And she was. I thought she was brave to slip on a swim suit and get on that stage, and to confront Scarlett Traina, and I thought she was brave for eating that corn-dog, because as silly as it sounds, I knew how much she hated and feared calories and this was an important moment.

"I want to do something good with my life," she said.

"I do, too," I said.

"I wanted to play football for Ole Miss," Daddy said, "but it didn't work out."

"It didn't work out because you never finished high school, and besides that you were too small for the team to begin with," Mama said. "I had dreams, too, you know. I wanted to be a singer and marry Frank Sinatra."

I looked at Daddy, trying to gage his reaction. He didn't seem to have one, maybe he was used to hearing his wife talk about wanting to marry a star.

Mama caught me looking at Daddy and realized what she had said. "The point is, trying to be something good can eat you alive. You just have to try your hardest to be happy with what you've got."

Mama had said the wrong thing. Ava pushed her second corn-dog away. I put mine down. I lost my appetite.

"I'm happy a good bit of the time," Daddy said. "Football season is the best. Frank Sinatra's music cheers me up."

"Me too," Mama said. "I've got my family. That's all I need to make me happy."

"Sinatra and football and my family. That's all I need. You girls just have dreams that are too big. You'll outgrow that."

"I know I did," Mama said, and she took Ava's second corn-dog and started eating it. "And I'm perfectly happy. Wanting is what eats at you. It will eat you inside and out."

"I've actually known desire to kill men. Grown men," Daddy said.
"I think it killed Spencer Frank, remember him, Rodney?"

"I know it killed him."

Somewhere at the far end of the bowling alley, a woman called her boyfriend a pig. She slapped him and his friends howled, amused by their buddy's embarrassment. A cocktail waitress dropped a glass in the bar and it shattered. The bartender rang a bell because someone just gave him a good tip. Mama moaned, delighting as the corn-dog filled her momentary need.

This bowling alley cacophony connected each of us in the place, like some Deep South ending to A Christmas Carol, where Scrooge rushes through the street wishing merriment and spirit on everyone in sight. At this moment, every one of us at the Dixie Spirit was united because we chose this place, of the limited number of destinations in Newitville, and were all participants in the experience.

I looked around at all the people — fat and tall, skinny, short, dressed in ratty jeans and old t-shirts, all the cheap bad haircuts —and I inhaled the mingled scent of various drugstore colognes. I wanted to go home and get in bed and never get out. I thought about fate, and how it alone made my parents' genes mix and produce me. I could have been born to an educated, rich family in Manhattan, and somehow, even with this DNA, I understood the advantages and privileges I would have gotten. Maybe I would have been tall with a straight nose and ample breasts. Instead, I was born to a family who bragged about giving up dreams and consoled themselves over losses in bowling alleys.

I looked at Ava, thinking she'd give me some sort of support, because I knew she had to be feeling just as bad, if not worse, having lost in the pageant. She was smiling, though, her eyes lighting on someone in the bar. I turned to see a guy with a thick brown shag and Jesus-blue eyes smiling back at her. He raised his drink and winked. She turned pink and looked down, still smiling.

"Excuse me," she said, getting up. "I need to go to the ladies room."

I watched my sister walk to the restroom. She swayed more than usual; she swayed more than she did on stage earlier. She strutted, she performed like earlier, but with more enthusiasm because she knew a man was watching.

The pageant was behind her, all those weeks of wanting and prepping for the crown. I could tell by the way she walked, by the way she had blushed, it would be a long time before my sister became the type of person who didn't need anything more than Sinatra and football.

It would even take more than a corn-dog to make her happy. She felt too pretty for wanting little things like that.

Chapter Five
I Was a Teenage Codependent!

A mistake had to have been made. I always believed this. I did not belong to this family. I had been switched by accident at the hospital or maybe I was adopted and the family conspired to keep it from me.

A side effect of this belief is that I went through strange stages growing up. For example, when I was five, I liked to crouch under the kitchen table during dinner and bark like a dog. A couple years later, I went through a shoplifting stage. I kept sticking things in my mother's purse, like once while we stood in line at a cash register I shoved a pack of Dentyne in her white handbag. She kept finding things, clueless as to where they came from, convinced she was losing her mind. That went on till she caught me in the Piggly Wiggly slipping more Dentyne into her purse.

She did not believe in spanking children, but Grandma did. I got switched with a strong twig from the switch tree in the backyard.

At ten I pretended to speak French. My entire family thought I had gone insane. Someone would ask me a simple question, like, "Lisa, how are you today?" and I would respond with nasal gibberish, throwing in (what I considered to be) common French words like "crepe," "bonjour" and "poodle."

Most of these phases unnerved my mother and sent her into the bathroom for a highball. Grandma, use to odd family behavior, simply included me in her prayers at night by saying, "Please let the child grow up to act right in the head and marry well." At each of my stages, Grandpa mumbled something about me being a "senseless kid," while Daddy just shook his head sadly, asking me from time to time if I acted kooky because I watched too much television.

Truth is, I did these things to rattle the adults. What else would I do for amusement? We had no neighbors, really, none with kids. Until I was in the fourth grade, the nearest neighbor was an eccentric old man, Mr. Schuman, who lived alone in a house with his ducks. He kept a tub full of water for them, and though I always wanted to go over and visit the ducks, Grandma wouldn't allow it.

The other neighbors lived a half-mile down the road. They were an elderly black couple who did not have a car, and used a mule and buggy to get into town. The sight of archaic transportation scared me, and whenever I was outside playing and heard that mule's hooves clopping on the pavement, I ran inside.

Living in a neighborhood with such strangeness, it's no wonder I went out of my way to be a little off. After a while these phases became a habit of sorts, a way to distinguish myself. When I got bored with one phase I'd move on, saying to myself, "Well, I've been speaking phony French for three weeks. What can I do now?"

By the time I reached fifteen I had refined my phases to the arts. I wrote short stories, mainly science fiction, where aliens swooped down in space ships and plucked up family members. I read these to my parents and grandparents for their amusement, they liked hearing their names in a story, as well as those of our cousins and aunts.

However, they were alarmed at the number of family abductions and experimental alien anal probes.

The phase that I loved the most had to be tap-dancing. I tap-danced frequently around the house although I never had even one lesson. My parents had paid for Ava to have tap, ballet, and piano training when she was young. They got mad when she quickly dropped out and vowed not to waste money on those kinds of things with me when I was old enough.

I was not deterred. Tap-dancing was not just any phase: I believed I had been born with a natural gift. Judging by the way I felt when I danced, I thought that gift was tap. I had decided early on to teach myself. I learned from TV, as I had spent much of the sixties and early seventies watching variety shows, and seeing everyone from Sammy Davis, Jr. to an aged Ginger Rogers tap, tap, tap across the screen.

As with my other phases, I did eventually grow weary of tap-dancing and had been thinking about working up a singing act, but I kept tapping for Mama's sake. My tap-dancing was the first thing that she really enjoyed, besides my short stories, which I also kept up, but not with great frequency as they required ineffable inspiration. The tap-dancing I could do anytime and it never failed to make Mama smile. Sometimes my short stories had no effect on her mood, as she had to think to follow them and her mind was usually focused on her "problem of the day." But with tap, all she had to do was watch me make a fool of myself. Presto, instant laughter.

And I needed to make her laugh — often. Mama always found reasons for trauma. Like, "It's Tuesday." Or "It's Wednesday." Or we were "Working-class," or she was "A tub of lard." Or, it was raining, it was too hot, too humid, and her husband harbored an immature love for Dinah Shore. Then there were the classic standards: she felt her own mother didn't love her, and her life had not turned out like she'd planned.

So instead of terminating my tap-dancing, I expanded my act. I sang, I danced, I told jokes. Sammy Davis, Jr. was my icon. I tried to catch all his TV variety show appearances. I mimicked the way he cracked up with his whole body, leaning over and putting his hands on his thighs and guffawing like he was trying to spit out a cat caught deep in his throat.

Because I continued writing stories, I started thinking pretentiously of myself as a renaissance girl, capable of all art forms. Except I did most things badly, as I had no training in anything. I couldn't spell worth a hoot and my stories were a challenge to read. My artistic talent seemed one step above an infant's. I was tone death, and therefore carrying a tune was as difficult as trying to perform brain surgery.

I had two good friends in high school. Monica Priestly and Tippi Blunt. I alternated between which one I considered my best friend. For most of my freshman and sophomore year, I considered Tippi the closer of the two. Monica had a boyfriend, which meant she was preoccupied most of the time.

I liked Tippi, too, because she reminded me of the Wizard in Emerald City, in that she knew things the rest of us didn't. In retrospect, she was a culture junkie, watching massive amounts of television, reading all sorts of magazines, from *Glamour* and *Cosmopolitan* to *Newsweek*, *Rolling Stone* and even *People*. She watched "Dick Frost," "Johnny Carson" and the "Today Show." She read books about people ranging from Ghandi to Charles Manson.

I am pretty sure she slept little. On the nights we had sleepovers with Monica, she kept us up, talking, telling us things, wild, useless things. David Bowie had different colored eyes because he had gotten into a fight as a teenager and someone stabbed him. Proper etiquette dictated that one ate asparagus with the fingers. Never wear white socks with pants. Montgomery Clift died in a car wreck after a dinner party at Elizabeth Taylor's house. James Dean was gay, Winston Churchill was an alcoholic, but he was so big he could drink more than most. If you flew around the earth backwards very fast you would go back in time, at least that was a theory. Aliens had landed in New Mexico during the forties but the government hid this from us.

She had all sorts of knowledge. She told me that the sky was blue because the atmosphere refracted the reflection of the oceans. I learned more from her than I did in science and history class put together.

Her mother was an armchair psychiatrist who read all the latest pop psychology and self-help books, like *I'm Okay, You're Okay*. Tippi read them too, taking them into the bathroom and sitting on the toilet for an hour, lost in theories and revelations.

It was Tippi who uncovered my real problem. It happened when I was spending the night at her house. Her mother was on a date; we were alone, something that would never happen in my house. I was pretty sure my parents and grandparents figured I needed a babysitter until I was married, as I was their precious commodity, their little peace maker, their short-story writing, tap dancing, singing entertainer. Tippi and I were in the living room, listening to her older brother's Steppenwolf album and eating some Jell-O chocolate pudding Mrs. Blunt had made for us.

I had just revealed another new plan of mine to fix my family emotionally before I went off to college. I believed it was the least I could do as a parting gift to the people who clothed and fed me. Which is how I thought of them: less like family, and more like kind benefactors as it was clear I was not really their blood relation but either a) adopted (why wouldn't they just tell me the truth?), or b) switched by accident at the hospital right after my birth.

"You're a co dependent," Tippi said, as casual as if she had just commented on the pudding.

"I'm a what?"

"I just read about it. Alcoholics need someone to validate their drinking. In a way, you do that for your mother by always cheering her up."

"What are you talking about?" I asked Tippi.

Tippi sat up and got her "overly patient" look on her face. I knew she was about to start doing this kind of "clinical talk" where she would speak slowly and pronounce each word carefully.

"You are the codependent child of an alcoholic. You are an unwitting partner for your mother. She can make a mess and you will clean it up. The term is mainly used in association with alcoholics, but you act in that capacity for all of your family. Your grandmother can get away with carping at your mother because she knows you'll come tap-dancing along and make everyone laugh. Same with your father and grandfather. They don't have to get in the middle of your mother and grandmother because you do. You put on your little shows and make everything okay."

At first it sounded like Tippi was just being mean. But after she fell asleep, I stayed awake thinking about what she had said. She gave a term to what I had known all along. I wasn't the peacemaker. I really was a teenage codependent.

And I had to stop the craziness.

For two weeks I did not sing, tap-dance, tell a joke or anything. I stayed in my bedroom and listened through the thin walls as my grandmother and mother had six fights in the kitchen, all variations on the same theme. Grandma was mad because Mama had been such a beautiful young lady and now she looked twenty years older than her actual age, Mama couldn't talk or walk straight at night after a few cocktails and her bedroom was a mess. If it weren't for Grandma, we'd live like rats. Et cetera.

In every fight Mama would yell something back, her voice cracking. Sometimes Daddy would yell from his chair in the living room, "Would you two please stop your hen fight?"

One night, Grandpa was in the kitchen when this happened. "Damn bastard, I'm gonna pop him one good!"

Grandma screamed, "Shut your mouth. I don't need you to fight my battles."

Grandpa harrumphed and shuffled into their room to watch the Carol Burnett show. I hated to miss that show, but I stayed cloistered in my room.

I did not come out even when Mama fled to the bathroom for a conciliatory cocktail and cried through the walls. I did not come out when Daddy, also in ear shot of her crying, slapped his hands against the arms of his easy chair and said, "Goddamned silly women, I wish to God they would stop this." I did not go out when I heard Grandma, through the other wall, scream to Grandpa, "THAT CHILD IS KILLING ME WITH HER DRINKING AND SHE CAN'T SEE WHAT SHE'S DOING!" and Grandpa screamed back, "WHAT?"

After two weeks, I had zits on my forehead and I had lost weight, not good since I was not developed at all. I overheard a woman at the mall say to her husband, "Look at that long-haired boy carrying a purse."

My home life was a mess and I felt bad about my looks. In retrospect, I was no different from any other kid, but at the time, you could not have convinced me of that. Tippi, with size 34-B breasts and a bubble butt that got the boys' attention, tried to console me with statistics. "Did you know that 96 percent of teenage girls feel bad about their body? Fascinating fact, 98 percent of adult women wish they looked like a model. So it will just get worse." Somehow, she meant that to cheer me up. She also told me that 49 percent of teenagers hated their family life. This was also meant to cheer me, but the message I got instead was, "51 percent of teenagers loved their family life. You're in the minority!"

I started getting insane ideas, like I would go live with Ava, who now lived in Bogalusa, Louisiana. It was the kind of town stuck in 1953. Black people still sat at the back of the bus and were relegated to the movie balcony as if somehow desegregation had spread through the South but missed this place. The one movie theater played second runs, no new releases. A typical ambition for a Bugalousa girl my age was to not get pregnant before she finished high school.

Still, I guess I was desperate enough that I called Ava one day from Mama and Daddy's bedroom phone.

"Can I come live with you?" I asked when she answered.

"No."

"Please."

"Is it that bad?"

"Yes. I've stopped tap dancing and it's gotten worse."

"Why did you do that?"

"Because I'm a teenage codependent."

"Oh." She didn't question what this meant. Maybe she knew, or maybe she wasn't listening because right about then, she started yelling at her two-year-old, Lucy, who had just put a lizard on the cat's back.

"I have to go," she said. "You don't want to live here. You'd have to sleep on the couch and Lucy would drive you nuts. She drives me nuts. She can be real bad, let me tell you. She needs someone to discipline her."

We hung up and I knew she was right about me moving in with her. My only shred of hope sunk as I thought ahead to the end of my senior year. It seemed too far away. But I had to stay strong. I was on to something. By going cold turkey on my codependent behavior, I believed I could make my family right.

And that night, I got some hope back. During their kitchen fight, Mama didn't cry: she just said, "Oh please, not tonight," and walked away from Grandma. It was progress. Maybe by weaning myself from being the entertaining peacekeeper, our family would have a breakthrough.

After they had all gone to bed, I didn't hear any mumbling through the walls. Everyone slept, and I slept too, confident we were on our way to being fixed.

My enthusiasm was short-lived. The next night, Mama had a drink after work with the ladies from the Heart of Dixie Museum. It was Blanche Smith's birthday. They went to the Satellite Lounge out on Highway 80 for strawberry daiquiris.

Mama came home, her mood smoothed by the rum. She went straight to the bathroom and smoothed her mood further with a couple of highballs. Grandma called my parents for dinner and while Daddy ate pork chops with vigor, Mama fell asleep in her seat. Grandma, who always ate with Grandpa before we did, happened to pass through the kitchen and see her. Her blood did a rapid boil and she spat, "God-damn whiskey," then slammed the door to her bathroom.

She ran a hot bath, trying to cool off, but I could hear her ranting about the evils of alcohol and how it had ruined her child and was breaking her heart. I imagined her soaking in her large claw-foot tub, underneath a naked light bulb. Just comparing her austere bathroom to my parents' bad Vegas lounge/bathroom summed up the differences between the warring parties.

Daddy came a bit undone by Grandma's quick and angry percolation. He shoved Mama in the arm and said, "Get your ass in bed."

"I'm just tired, Sug," Mama said, which is what she always said whenever we accused her of being drunk.

She put on her nightgown and returned to the living room and said, "I think I want to watch some television." She sat in her easy chair and pulled her knees up to her chest. Pretty soon she was snoozing, mouth open, nightgown hiked above her knees and, not wearing panties, her hidden treasures revealed to the world.

I didn't witness any of this, though I heard the whole thing from my room, where I had been reading up on West Coast colleges. I learned the visual details later from my grandmother, who repeated the story often to me over the years, as an example of how low one can sink from drink.

Pretty soon, Grandma came out of the bathroom and saw Mama's secret treasures from the kitchen. She walked into the living room and said to Daddy, "You're just going to let her sit like that?"

"She's fine, leave her alone. She ain't hurting no one."

"She's a disgrace."

"Leave her alone."

The conversation continued. Grandma said Mama was vulgar and a disgrace. Daddy told her to mind her own business. Grandpa even got involved because they were so loud.

"Don't talk to her that way," He yelled at Daddy about Grandma.

"Don't talk to me, old man. I've worked hard today and I don't want any of this shit."

Mama was passed out during all this, amazingly enough. My feet started twitching. I envisioned me running out into the living room and bursting into tap. They would laugh and go away. But I couldn't. They had to learn for themselves; they could not continue with this behavior.

I heard a thrack. Someone hit someone, and to this day, I'm not sure what happened, but I think Grandma slapped Mama's legs.

"Put on some drawers," she yelled.

Mama woke, startled, "Whaaa . . .?"

"You're showing your nether regions. It's disgusting."

"Please Mama," my mother begged, confused from her nap.

"You're drinking is getting worse. It's one thing to do it in the house, but now your taking it to the bars."

"It was Blanche's birthday."

"You could have bought her a gift other than liquor. It's not enough that you have to be a lush, but now your friends have to be one, too?"

Daddy started yelling "That's enough," and Grandpa shot in, "Watch your tone." Soon everyone was yelling and I could not take it. I ran into the living room and I started tap dancing and singing like no one has ever tapped-danced or sang.

My feet were gun fire and I waved my arms in titanic circles. My eyes were the size of confessionals and pleaded for peace. My tongue triple wagged I sang so hard.

Mama sat in her chair, crying into her hands, rocking back and forth, sobbing in a high-pitched hyena voice, "Why do you hate me, Mama? Why can't you see how hard I work? I just get tired, that's all."

And Daddy yelled, "For God's sake, go back to your room and stop acting like a clown."

And Grandma said, "See what you've done, your daughter feels like she has to act like a moron just to keep you sober. She's not right in the head because you drank during labor with her."

And Mama cried, "Oh hell, I drank the whole time I was pregnant. She's fine. She's just trying to make you stop yelling at me."

And Grandpa said, "Is that true, you blame your grandmother for this?"

But I couldn't answer him. My feet were tapping, faster and faster. Any moment now, they would blast off from my legs and jettison to the moon. My arms, stuck in a wild revolution, were on the brink of busting out of my shoulders and flapping after my feet. I sang Sinatra so loud that at any second, all the glass in Newitville would shatter.

"I've got you under my skin, I've got you, deep in the heart of me . . ."

Chapter Six
Lost in the Cosmos

In 1976, when I was sixteen, Jimmy Castelli tried to convince me to lose my virginity.

"You will if you love me," he said. Jimmy and I had been boyfriend and girlfriend for three months. I thought I might love him, and for sure knew I needed him the way a swamp needs muck to qualify as a swamp. He was cute and popular, and had once dated Tracy Howell, the head cheerleader. Just by virtue of being his girlfriend, I went from being an in-crowd has been to an up and coming player on the high school scene in Newitville. People who once scorned me treated me like I was the hot new kid on the scene, scouting membership in my exclusive club.

We were parked next to Rattlesnake Lake in his old midnight blue 1970 Dodge Charger. It was April and the summer heat had crept in during the last week. I wore a sundress and no hose, a choice of clothes which Jimmy evidently interpreted as a subtle offer to explore my body. So he sang a teenage lover's plea in my ears, as I pushed his hand from all my girlie places, fighting to remain pure, a Southern female's main asset.

"I could have sex with someone else, but you wouldn't want that, Lisa. I know the first time is special; I just can't keep waiting. It's different for guys. We can't help ourselves. It's painful for us not to have sex."

"I think I might be too young, Jimmy."

"The thing is, it will clear up your acne."

"I don't have acne."

"Yeah, but you will if you don't have sex. Your glands get clogged."

"Huh?"

"Come on, Lisa, take a chance. Be brave."

I was not that brave. I resisted that night, but lost it the next Wednesday afternoon. We did it at Tippi Blunt's house, in the guest room on the bed next to a pile of clean clothes that needed ironing. The board was set up, the iron unplugged. The housekeeper didn't come on Wednesdays.

A couple years later, during my college freshman year, I read a book by Walker Percy, *Lost in the Cosmos*. Percy mused that what defines us is how we spend our average Wednesday afternoon. What did we do with our time?

I thought about my mother as I lost my virginity to Jimmy that Wednesday afternoon. I could see her face, disapproving, ashamed. I didn't feel anything but guilt, and a slight prick down below when Jimmy broke through. No pun intended.

When I read *Lost in the Cosmos*, I thought back to that afternoon, and it seemed right, appropriate even, given my family and the way we were most of the time. On any ordinary day of the week we did extraordinary things, like the Tuesday morning before I lost my virginity.

That day, Mama got drunk at lunch. She enjoyed a liquid meal of straight Jack Daniel's at PJ's Last Chance across the Mississippi River. She was driving Daddy's spare truck because the Belle-Mobile, her murky brown Cordova, was in the auto repair shop getting a new gasket.

On her way back to work, she blacked out and plunged the truck through the Burger Chef on Lee Street in downtown Newitville. The truck burst through the large, welcoming wall-of-windows at the front of the burger palace. Mama finally braked and the vehicle stopped shy of the counter. Fortunately, no one was hurt. Even the truck survived okay, with just dents and scratches in the hood.

Mama should have spent time in jail for this. But the Newitville sheriff was a good pal of Grandpa's. They both swore communists were ruining America. They talked about it in detail once a week in the parking lot outside the Sally Sunflower Supermarket. Grandpa and a small gang of friends, almost all WW I veterans (except for the sheriff, who was WW II), gathered there every Tuesday to eat fresh French Horns from the bakery section. In between pastry bites, they pitched a bitch over the way communists and unions were sending our country to hell in a hand-basket.

They were doing just that when the sheriff got the call on his radio, announcing that Mama had created a new drive-through window at the Burger Chef.

Grandpa, mad that his daughter had embarrassed him in front of his friends, drove home and lit what would be the first of many trash fires right in the center of our driveway. It was his way of discouraging Mama and Daddy from coming home — ever. He threw the match on the trash, which he had soaked in gas, just as my parents were about to drive up the driveway. Unfortunately, he created the pile too close to a plum tree and almost instantaneously it burst into a fiery blaze.

We had a new neighbor who had just built a house across the road. Mrs. Warren. She must have been schizophrenic, or had some clinically emotional disorder. Grandpa said she just wasn't right in the head. All I knew was that she had to be medicated and on that day, had evidently not taken her pills. When she saw the burning tree, she got all biblical and ran out into the middle of the road in her slip and bra, screaming, "Burning bush, burning bush. God's arrived! God's arrived!"

The sheriff and fire department were summoned. Everyone within a mile of our home on Gnarled Branch Road walked down to view the blaze as well as witness Mrs. Warren's nervous breakdown. Dogs barked like madmen baying in a rainstorm. Mama, sleeping off her drunken stupor, was oblivious in the front seat of Daddy's work van, which he had now parked on the side of the road.

Daddy and Grandpa stood in the driveway and had a cussing match. Grandma broke up the fight by beating them with a broom. Clancy Miller, a reporter for the *Newitville Evening Post*, took copious notes. I stayed in my room and listened to Bruce Springsteen's latest album, *Darkness on the Edge of Town*, which seemed appropriate given the situation. I used headphones so I didn't have to hear my family's version of civil disobedience enacted outside my window.

The sheriff put Mrs. Warren in jail. Grandpa said he hated crazy people. They were ruining this country along with the communists and unions. Mama, due to Grandpa's friendship with the sheriff, went unscathed by the law.

Unfortunately, every episode of the day — Mama's lunch-time ride, Grandpa's trash-burning/plum tree destruction, and Mrs. Warren's breakdown —made the paper. The *Newitville Evening Post* was not used to printing such dramas, and Clancy Miller went all out, showing how Mama's lunch time imbibing caused a chain reaction.

My father was quoted as saying, "It's been a bad day for our family."

Grandma, also made the paper. "Booze is ruining more than just my family, it's ruining this damn nation." She went on to blame liquor for unwed mothers, unemployment, crime, unions, communism and even spider veins. But mainly communists. "It's a known fact that all those Russians are drunks."

At which point Grandpa muttered to Clancy, "Goddamned communists. Country's going to hell in a hand-basket."

The *Newitville Evening Post*, being a family paper, ran my grandparents cusswords in cartoon type. Grandma's "damn" became: "D@!n." For Grandpa's GD word, they wrote, "G#%*d!$&d."

Ava and I were the only ones in the family who didn't make the paper. Ava, who still lived in Bogalusa, Louisiana, was ignorant of the day as it was a safe four hours drive from Newitville. Bogalusa had only one television station, which came out of Ruston, another small town and also far enough away not to carry news of Newitville. She wouldn't have known about anything, except I called to tell her.

Really, I had an ulterior motive. I wanted to ask her advice about Jimmy, but when she heard the news about Mama and Grandpa and Mrs. Warren, she said, "Oh Jesus Christ. I can't take too much more of this hullabaloo. Honest. I need a drink and I don't even drink. These people can't drive me far enough away!"

Given the mood she was in, I didn't think the time was right to discuss whether or not her sixteen-year-old sister should be doing the big monkey.

Losing your virginity should be extraordinary; after all, you only get to lose it once. But given the events of that Tuesday, it didn't seem that way to me. On Wednesday everyone looked at me all day like I was some sort of fresh freak because my mother made Burger Chef into a drive-through and my grandfather was a plum tree arsonist. Overnight Mama had developed a reputation as The Town Drunk. If I wasn't a freak myself, I sure felt like I came from a family of them.

The only other person at school who hit the grapevine with any force was Savanna Cruz, the school slut. She had just slept with Michael Massey, the quarterback for the Trojans, our football team. But people looked at her with a reverence reserved for rock stars. I even caught Jimmy eyeing her in the cafeteria. He and Tippi had been my only real friends that day, the two people who would talk to me and act like things were normal at my house.

When he stared at Savanna, I said, "She did it with Michael Massey," and he said, "Mmm hmmm," like he wasn't really listening, like his mind was far off somewhere. He had this slight smile on his face, like he had just slurped down some damn good ice cream.

I knew by the dreamy look in his eyes that if I didn't do something fast, and I mean fast, I could whittle my newly reduced list of friends down to just Tippi. So that afternoon, in the Blunt's guest bedroom, next to the pile of clean clothes, I thought about the article in the *Newitville Evening Post* and how Clancy was right about chain reactions. Life could be so much like dominoes. Stand them up and tip one over; it sets off all the others. Mama gets drunk in the morning and click, click, click, I'm losing my virginity in an attempt to keep my horny boyfriend out of Savanna Cruz's pants.

Jimmy and I broke up a month later. We were supposed to meet one Saturday night at McDonalds. I waited an hour for him to show, then called Tippi from the pay phone.

"Jimmy stood me up," I said.

"That bastard!" She was a good friend, always jumping to take my side without knowing the facts. For all we knew, he could have been smeared on the highway pavement after a bad accident. We just assumed the worst, though.

"He's cheating on me," I said.

"That son of a bitch! Get over here. Let's go find him."

"Where?"

"Where else? Rattlesnake Lake."

Rattlesnake Lake existed for the dual purpose of giving Newitville teenagers an opportunity to express their love to their sweethearts, and to cheat on each other.

I picked up Tippi and we drove to Rattlesnake Lake, which sat on the far edge of the subdivision where she lived. We slowly cruised by all the cars. The shock of bare flesh greeted us at every window; strangers' bodies engaged in front seat ballets.

Sure enough, we passed Jimmy's Charger. I had half expected to catch him with Savanna Cruz. It would be so like her to steal another girl's boyfriend. But I was in for a surprise. Jillian Preston, Savanna's best friend, sat topless in Jimmy's front seat. Her breasts brazenly beamed through the illicit dark of his car. All I could see of Jimmy was a gob of his blond hair, as her breast encased his face. The Charger's radio dial, shining radioactive green, reflected against the back of his head. I wondered what they were listening to, and for some reason, probably in a self-pitying attempt to make the moment even worse, I thought of that old song, "Be My Baby."

Jillian Preston was the type of girl who jiggled her whole being; from her bouncy blonde hair and her huge breasts to her ample butt and thighs. She drove a cherry red Volkswagen Bug. It seemed the right kind of car for her. She was as cute as the car and giggly as cherry red can make a person feel. But of course, red is also a universal color for danger, which may have been the cosmos's way of being ironic when it came to Jillian.

It didn't take me long to get over Jimmy. I did it by throwing myself into a simmering obsession I had with Bruce Springsteen, the Boss of Rock and Roll. He was my true love, always, but it somehow abated whenever I had a boyfriend.

"Really, I don't know what I was thinking," I told Tippi. "I should have saved myself for Bruce."

"You would probably have had to save yourself for an awfully long time," Tippi pointed out.

It didn't deter me that Bruce was the savior of rock and roll. I understood that getting to meet him, much less getting to know him, would be tricky. But I vowed never to even look at another guy. I would just concentrate on getting out of Newitville, and moving to New York or LA or somewhere fabulous. I'd be a writer of such wild, insane success that Bruce's knees would knock at the mere thought of meeting me.

I was still writing short stories. Unfortunately, I had developed the delusion that my work had some sort of raw, edgy inspiration. In time, I believed I would improve vastly, beyond belief. I would equal Faulkner (whom I had heard was the greatest, but hadn't read), or even surpass him.

Years later, I would remember that the critics lauded Bruce's music as raw, edgy, and inspired. I now know I had what I have since labeled "plaudit transference." Which is believing someone else's acclaim describes you.

Another reason I quickly got over the heartache of Jimmy was that the people at school were starting to talk to me again. My family couldn't compare with the latest news. The homecoming queen, Lisa Burns, had slept with her brother, Hank. They did it on purpose, a consensual act. It seemed like a good idea, they thought, practicing on each other. That was the rumor.

Unfortunately, I could not be too ebullient over my restored social standing. I had a new anxiety.

It was a few days after Jimmy and I broke up.

A Wednesday.

Tippi and I were sitting on the lawn outside the chemistry lab eating celery sticks for lunch. She said we had to diet as we were size fours and needed to be size twos. I went along, though I was fairly sure that for me, it was fruitless given my feared condition. I had just realized that morning my period was a week late.

"I'm thinking of dying my hair red. Red's different, you know. Like Ann Margaret red," she was saying.

"I think I'm pregnant," I blurted and started to tear up.

Tippi choked on her celery. "This will not help your popularity," she managed to finally say.

"Lisa Burns seems to be doing fine," I said. "And look at what she's doing with her brother."

"Yeah, but to be blunt, she's really pretty. Maybe if you bleached your hair your popularity would survive. People like platinum blondes."

I should have been hurt by Tippi's comment, but that's the way she and I talked to each other. The good that happened to others happened because they were rich or attractive. If bad things happened to us, we just weren't trying hard enough. We had to be thinner or blonder or better dressed.

We learned by example, from the Savanna's and Jillian's and Lisa's. Although we stopped short of having sex with our brothers. Well, I didn't have a brother, but if I had one, I wouldn't have done that.

Fortunately for me, integration hadn't fully caught up with Newitville, Mississippi. Tippi drove me to Kuhn Memorial, the honest-to-God name of the "black" hospital in town. I always thought some old racist had named the hospital as a mean joke. I would hear the old whites in town disparaging blacks with the word "coon." Of course, the blacks in town had a few words for the whites, too, like "redneck freaks," "interbreeding jackasses," "honkey cooters."

That day, though, I didn't care if anyone called me a honkey or a sinner or anything as long as they didn't call me by my real name. I was just glad we had a hospital I could go to; no one in this hospital was likely to know my parents.

Still, it was a small town, and so instead of giving my real name to the front desk, I told them I was Maria Schwinn. This was Tippi's idea. She picked the name after the Schwinn bicycle. "If there are Schwinns anywhere, I think they are Canadian or something. No one will ever catch us," she said.

As bad luck would have it, Cassie Thomas, the smartest girl in my algebra class, was sitting in the waiting area with her mother. She was the top black student in school; in fact, she was the top student.

"What are you doing here?" she asked. She seemed displeased that people like us would be there — and not because we were white. Cassie was a snob who only associated with the other honor students. Tippi and I didn't have time to make straight A's; we had to settle for B's since we were busy trying to be thinner and more popular. I was strongly considering taking Tippi's advice and dying my hair platinum blonde, but I had this fear that if I did that, I'd start feeling guilty for being so shallow and not applying myself in stuff like History and English a little more. Maybe if I actually studied instead of focusing on being popular, I could nudge those B's to A's. Maybe then I could hope for more in life besides an education from Ole Miss.

Besides, those subjects were kind of interesting to me, and I had Cassie to thank for that. I liked the exchange of dialogue between her and the teachers in history class. Not only did she always know the answers to questions, but she would bring up certain additional points about events. She put things in context. In fact, she was the reason I knew the word "context." "You have to put Gettysburg in context," she said one day in class. That night, I broke out the dictionary and turned to the C's to look up context.

"I have a sore throat," I told Cassie, answering her question with a lie.

"She can't get rid of it," Tippi said.

"So you came here?"

We looked at her like we knew there was an implication, but we didn't get it. "Well, it's the closest hospital to home," I said in a tone that implied she was dense.

I picked up an issue of *Ebony* and started reading an article on Richard Pryor. Tippi picked up another *Ebony*. Secretly, we were annoyed that there were only black magazines on the waiting room table, and whispered our irritation to each other.

"I mean, that's kind of racist, don't you think?" Tippi whispered.

"Yes I do."

Cassie heard us and slanted her eyes. "This *is* the black hospital," she said.

"Actually, it's a federally funded hospital," Tippi said. "It's for poor people."

"That's who the poor *are* in this town. *Black*." Then Cassie looked over at me and cocked her head. "Speaking of poor, how's your poor mother by the way?"

"Great," I said with alacrity, my mouth stretched into a sunbeam to cover what I really felt. "She's super. Fine. Fine. Fine. Whole family is terrific."

The truth is I had come to think of my family as pages in an old book coming unglued at the spine. During the next few days, as I waited for my test results, I would become one of those loose pages. I would fall out, unnoticed on the floor, a sheer slippery danger for someone to step on and lose their footing.

Mama decided we needed to have The Talk. "Birds, bees. That stuff," she said.

Somehow, I thought mistakenly, she knew about Jimmy. She knew I could be carrying the next generation of Tingle in my skinny womb.

She sat me down in her bathroom, during happy hour.

Daddy was at the VFW for men's night, which seemed like a misnomer to me: all nights at the VFW were men's nights except for Thursday, when they were allowed to bring their wives for potluck night. So it was just me and Mama in the bathroom. She poured herself a light highball. I use the word light because that's how she put it. "I need to cut back on my drinking, sugar, because frankly, that's why I've called you in here. I'm pregnant."

For a disoriented moment, I thought she meant I was pregnant, and she knew about Jimmy. I was surprised that she was so calm, that she had not unleashed the wrath of God, or Grandma, on me. Then the words sunk in and I blurted out, "Oh, *you're* pregnant."

"Well, who did you think I was talking about?"

"You're what?"

"You do understand about babies right? I mean, you have a good idea how they come into the world."

"Yes, the stork."

Mama looked pale. She didn't want to have to go into detail. This was a talk she had never prepared for.

"Mama, babies come from two people having sex, and yes, I understand sex. I watch television."

She jiggled her drink and took a sip, then pointing her finger my way said, "Thank God. Your grandmother is always saying we let you watch too much television, but I told her you were learning things."

There wasn't much more to the conversation. Mama said she expected the baby to arrive in seven months judging by her belly. She had to see the doctor to confirm. So far all she had done was take one of those at-home pregnancy tests, but she had taken it three times to make sure. Plus, she knew the signs: fatigue, aches, like you are about to get a cold but never do, nausea and a general sense that your life is about to change irrevocably.

"They have at-home pregnancy tests now?" I asked as that realization hit me.

"Well sure! You can get them at Walgreens!"

"Shit," I said, thinking about all the trouble and trauma Tippi and I went through to go to Kuhn Memorial. I could have known by now if I was pregnant or not.

"Watch your mouth, Lisa Tingle. What's wrong with you?"

"I'm just amazed at modern medicine, that's all."

"Don't I know it. It's a miracle."

I had a dream that night I will never forget. Mama and I were both pregnant. Of course, no one at school would talk to me, and as punishment for having sex, the principal put me back in sixth grade math and told me I had to start over from there.

Like most dreams, it consisted of random clips. The next thing I knew, Mama and I had both given birth, though that wasn't in the dream. It jumped to the next scene where my kid and Mama's, two girls, were in a playpen coloring. Even though they were just infants, they had a book of standard child stuff: images of clouds, trees, flowers, birds, cows.

My kid colored the cloud black, the tree red, the flowers brown, and the birds and cow purple. Mama's kid couldn't stay in the lines. My kid got mad over Mama's child's ineptness and hit her over the head with the coloring book. Then my girl started pounding her little fist all over Mama's girl.

Mama and I just stood back and watched, shrugging our shoulders. Mama said, "Well what can we do?" and I said, "I don't know."

I had another strange dream a few nights later. Again, I had a baby girl. In one scene, she's a fat kid that I don't know what to do with and don't particularly want. In the next scene my baby is a dog, and not just any dog. She has been dipped in batter and deep-fried like chicken. But the dog/baby is still alive and running around, her crusty skin falling off in juicy flakes. To this day, I will not eat fried chicken.

I'm sure those dreams had something to do with the anxiety I felt at the time. As for the first dream, the babies were probably an extension of Mama and me. As a kid I used strong dark colors in my art projects. My mother was a messy person, so the fact that her kid could not color inside the lines doesn't surprise me.

As for the second dream, well, that had to have been a subconscious statement regarding my general teenage angst. Pregnancy made you fat. Fried chicken (enough of it) could make you fat. To a teenage girl in Newitville, fat held as large a stigma as being pregnant. Hence, fried baby/dog/chicken dreams.

I called the hospital a few days after I had taken the blood test, and asked for the nurse who had attended to me.

"This is Maria Schwinn," I said. "Do you have my test results?"

"We lost them for a few days, actually. But we finally found them," she said, and then paused like she was about to announce the winner of an award. "Under the name Lisa Tingle."

"Oh. Umm. Ugh. Hmm."

"Mmm hmm. Relax, you aren't pregnant. But if your period doesn't come soon, go see your regular doctor, you hear me?"

"Okay doke." I was trying to act casual, like I wasn't bothered by being a lying sinner who'd had premarital sex.

A thought struck me. "How did you know me?"

"Sugar, this is a small town, and just because you're white folk and I'm black folk and things are pretty segregated don't mean black folks aren't aware of who the white folks are. You go to school with my kid Nancy Tipton. You're next to each other in the yearbook."

"Oh."

"Let me ask you something. What would you have done if you were pregnant? Have an abortion?"

"I dunno." I didn't want to tell her the truth, that I would have had an abortion over in Jackson — this coming after I figured out how to get the three or four hundred dollars for the cost of the procedure.

"You dunno. I bet you are proud of yourself. Are you proud of yourself?"

"No ma'am."

"No. I didn't think so."

What I couldn't tell this woman, what she couldn't understand as she admonished me in her peculiar rhetorical questioning way was that my shame and lack of pride could not outweigh the mortification I would have endured over telling my family that their baby was about to birth a bastard. Two words, one quick stroke. "I'm pregnant." Boom, I would have murdered my Grandma and Mama, and given Daddy and Grandpa a good strong stroke.

I answered the nurse with a pensive, "Umm."

"Mmm hmm. That's why I always say, babies shouldn't have babies."

"I agree, Ma'am."

"You behave, child, from here on out, you hear? Don't be in such a hurry to grow up."

"Okay doke," I said, then thanked her and hung up.

Despite being caught in my ruse, I felt light. I don't think I had ever known true relief. I mean, I understood what the word meant, and I understood the relief from hunger after crash dieting all day and sinking my teeth into a McDonald's Fish Burger and shoving an order of fries into my mouth. But I didn't know emotional relief. I would not have to have an abortion.

I walked out into the backyard and looked up at the blue sky. I took a deep breath. The furry, airy bloom of a pussy willow floated past me. Our damp woods were filled with these plants. The sun lit up the fine white strands, it looked like a little universe gliding across the ether. I felt like it looked.

As it turned out, Mama was going through menopause. Finally, after sixteen years, when she first thought she was going through this, but instead was pregnant with me, the day had come.

She walked around the house saying, "I'm barely fifty and already I have to go through the change! Don't I have enough to worry about!"

Daddy asked her how it would affect their, "you know," and she said, "No, I don't know," and he whispered the words, "sex life." I could hear because my bedroom door was open and even with the television blaring, the walls were so thin it didn't matter. I had been so wrapped up in my possible pregnancy that the obvious hadn't occurred to me:

My parents still had sex.

"Look on the bright side," Tippi told me at school the next day. "At least you know that they love each other if they are still having sex."

The thought didn't help.

Mama's moods, always erratic, grew even more so. She cried at Kodak commercials or when Daddy asked her to pass the salt for his mashed potatoes. "Didn't I salt them enough?" she would ask.

He learned questions like this were a trial.

"Um. Yes?"

"Then why do you need more salt?"

They would stare at each other, him helpless to think up an answer.

"I like a lot of salt."

She would cry because after thirty years of marriage, he still didn't like her cooking.

Four months later, I still did not have my period. I finally told Mama.

"OH MY GOD, YOU AREN'T . . ." She stopped, "ARE YOU????"

"No ma'am."

Relieved, she said, "Well, maybe you're just anemic. Maybe you have cancer." Then she realized what she had just said. "Oh my God!" she started to cry.

We visited my doctor a few days later. It was a Wednesday afternoon. Again, it didn't seem extraordinary to me at the time. But even to this day, I think about Walker Percy's *Lost in the Cosmos* and I marvel that there I was on an average weekday, doing something as normal as going to the doctor. And Percy was right: it is what you do on a normal Wednesday afternoon that defines your character. In this case, it defined me and my mother's character. She wanted me to go to the doctor to discover if I was barren or had cancer, and I acquiesced.

"She's so thin and pale," Mama said to the doctor. She hardly eats. Honey, don't you want to eat something?"

"Nope," I said, swinging my legs under the exam table. "I just had an apple a few hours ago."

Mama withered in her shoes.

Dr. Bolden was my physician. I had recently put my crush on Bruce Springsteen on the back burner while I pursued a new crush on Dr Bolden's son, Max. He was a bear of a boy with eyes as light and airy as pussy willow. He made me laugh, but he loved Savanna Cruz. All boys loved Savanna Cruz and it must have been her destiny to be loved by all boys.

"Your body fat is too low," Dr. Bolden said. "You need to eat."

Mama was beside herself with relief. Yet still, she cried.

I was embarrassed, partly by her histrionics, but mainly at myself. All my efforts ended with irony. My actions were a chain of disastrous reactions. I worried about Savanna stealing my boyfriend, only to have him stolen by her jiggly best friend. I went to Kuhn Memorial and made up an elaborate lie so I wouldn't get recognized, only to find out I could have bought an at-home pregnancy test. Then, in an effort to be fabulous and popular I made myself sick by trying to always be thinner and thinner.

"So I'm going to be okay?" I asked. Then it hit me. What did low body fat mean? Could I die? I couldn't die. I wanted to date Max Bolden, grow up and write stunning works of literary achievement, and then marry Bruce Springsteen. I wanted to finally read Faulkner.

"If you keep this lunacy up, no, you won't be okay, you'll get very sick," Dr. Bolden said. "Eat more and you'll blossom like a rosebud. Promise me you'll go home and eat a steak."

Mama sobbed and said, "Promise the doctor you'll eat, baby, promise."

Casual, nonchalant, like I was okay, like the moment was the kind of moment that happened to me on any given Wednesday, I said to Dr. Bolden, "Okay doke."

Chapter Seven
Motion

The earth revolves around the sun, and the moon revolves around the earth. Comets shoot across space. Stars explode into existence and then eventually implode into blackness. All of the cosmos is in constant motion.

Down on Earth there is constant motion as well. I learned about the true laws of motion not from science, but from my hero, the man who I knew beyond a shadow of a doubt, absolutely, 100 percent, no question about it, I would one day marry.

Bruce Springsteen, my rock and roll savior: the man who glorified the art of Getting Out in song.

I guess I spoiled Thanksgiving for my family my senior year of high school by professing my unrequited love for Bruce to my parents and grandmother. They were quite surprised, stunned even. I don't know why. They had to have suspected I had feelings for the man. My bedroom walls were covered with his posters. My night table was a stack of *Rolling Stones*, which I bought just to read tidbits on him in "Random Notes." When *Time* and *Newsweek* both ran Bruce on their cover in the same week, an event that at the time made rock and roll history, I framed the photos. I spent my allowance on his records. I wore Bruce Springsteen t-shirts. How, how could my family not realize that I was deeply, madly, fanatically-scary in love with the man?

My confession came during dinner. Grandpa was in bed with a bad cold. Grandma joined my parents and me at the table. It was actually a cheery occasion. Mama seemed happy to have her mother join us, as my grandparents never sat at the table when Daddy was present. Mealtime resembled a Basque restaurant with two seatings: Grandma and Grandpa's; Mama and Daddy's.

Grandma was also happy from a hard day spent doing what she loved, cooking. Our dinner table looked like a picture out of *Southern Living* magazine. We had oyster cornbread dressing, a fat smoked Butterball turkey, green bean casserole, cranberry mold, Parker House rolls, candied sweet potatoes, mashed potatoes, and carrot soufflé, which was basically mashed carrots. Things were going well. I remember sitting there thinking that something was off, then I realized we looked like some normal family from television.

But it didn't last long. Like I said, I myself ruined the occasion. When Grandma held the gravy bowl up and asked me, "Do you want gravy?" I felt the sudden need to respond with, "No, I want Bruce Springsteen."

She put the bowl down. Daddy grunted. Mama said, "Oh na-uh, that's not right, you shouldn't be having those kinds of thoughts about boys, not at your age, missy."

"You're too young to be liking boys," Daddy said .

"I'm seventeen!"

"Listen to you wasting your time on silly fantasies," Grandma shook her head. She tisked, which seemed unnecessarily dramatic.

"Grandma, you don't know if it's silly or not. You don't even know Bruce."

"And neither do you. That damn boy is probably a drug addict. It would break your grandpa's heart to know you've got a crush on a drug-using, rock and roll singer."

"You're talking again like Grandpa's dead, Grandma." It was true. She had started speaking of him in the past tense, I'm sure, to prepare herself for his eventual fate. Grandpa was running up against ninety, and Grandma treated his every ache as if he had already died. When he caught his recent cold, I was sure she had opened up the phone book and memorized the number of the funeral home, just in case.

"Don't mention death and your grandfather in the same breath!" She said.

"But you act like he's already, you know. Gone."

"Now Doodie, you are just being rude," Mama scolded. "I guess you get that behavior from those rock and roll magazines you read."

"That Bruce is greasy looking, Doodie," Daddy said.

"You know," Mama pointed her fork at me, "this is very troubling. What if that boy is the type of man you are always going to go for? I heard on Phil Donahue that some girls always fall for hoodlums because they have low self-esteem."

"Mama, did Phil Donahue actually say the word 'hoodlums' on TV, or is that your word?"

"Don't change the subject," Mama said, and stuck a bite of turkey into her mouth. Between chews, she asked, "How's your self-esteem?"

"Tell me how yours is and I'll tell you how mine is."

She swallowed and scraped up a lob of mashed potatoes. "This is not funny." Mama didn't look up. "Na-uh."

"Your mother had a thing for Sinatra," Daddy said. "It damn nearly busted us up. I'm telling you now, a crush on a star is a bad thing. It's not right. Look at what happened to your sister."

During the sixties Ava had a crush on Paul McCartney. When he married Linda Eastman, Ava stayed in bed for two weeks and declared her life "ruined." She lost a lot of weight, too much in fact. She wasn't one to make good grades, but they slipped even further. My parents were summoned to the principal's office. He wanted to put Ava in the slow-learners program with all the true hoodlums, as well as those that had real learning disabilities.

Everything turned out okay, though, because Ava liked being in the slow learners group. She said she felt superior to the others because their lives were much more messed up, and they liked her because she was different from them, in a positive way. Ava had a larger vocabulary (well, at least she knew tenth grade level words, like "vocabulary") and didn't have a jail record. She started to put on a little weight, got a boyfriend, and Paul became a distant memory.

But still, *still*, I could tell that when she heard a Beatles song on the radio, Paul was under her skin, burrowed, with no chance she'd ever completely dispel him.

I had no intentions of getting all anorexic or dive-bombing my grades over a broken heart because, frankly, Bruce and I were different from Ava and Paul, or Mama and Sinatra. We were meant to be together. So when Daddy compared me to Mama and Ava, I looked him straight in the eye and quoted my new favorite personal anthem "Badlands," written by Bruce, of course.

I finished reciting the lyrics, and my family responded with complete silence around the table.

Grandma stabbed a knife through the mound of cranberry mold on her plate. Daddy just looked at me, his lips a fine seam. Mama blinked.

"It's my mantra," I said. "Bruce wrote it, but I could have easily written it myself. It sums me up."

More silence. Grandma stuck a forkful of the cranberry mold in her mouth and chewed like she was trying to kill with her teeth. She swallowed, and after another angst-filled pause, said. "Lord almighty, I have never understood the fascination you Tingles have with stars. You'd think your own life isn't good enough."

"Well it's not," I said.

Mama's jaw dropped. Grandma's eyes slit to a furious sliver. Daddy's face turned the color of a strangled beet. Nothing could make him angrier quicker than someone passing judgment on him. "If it's good enough for me, then it's good enough for you," he said.

"Life is all about change. If things stay the same, you just wither away."

"Oh Jesus," Daddy turned to Mama. "She's been reading nonsense again."

"Baby, you should watch more television. I think those books and magazines you like to read are bad for you," Mama said.

"I didn't read that," I said. "I thought it up on my own." Actually, I didn't know if that was true. Maybe I had read it; maybe I had dreamt it. Or possibly I had an extra gene the rest of my family didn't have, and I was therefore born with the thought.

"Listen to your mama, I know, Doodie, believe me, I know what it's like to have a crush on some star. I went through that with Sinatra. It's fun, but it can torture you, too."

"I don't have a simple crush on Bruce. Call it what you will, but I have a connection with him formed by his music. The music makes what I feel special."

"Please baby," Mama said, "don't start thinking you're different and special. That's how you'll end up heartbroken."

What was it about Bruce that made me love him so? I think it was the way his songs evoked movement — as in me moving away from my crazy home and Newitville. I would lie on my bed with my headphones strapped around my head and, and listen to *Born to Run* or *Darkness on the Edge of Town*. I'd think about how the whole world existed in motion, like the way the earth revolved around the sun and the moon around the earth and so on. And out on a lonely highway, just like in Bruce's song "The Promised Land," some guy in a car was "driving that dusty road from Monroe to Angeline" and points beyond. It didn't matter the destination; it was the getting away, the getting on, *the going* that counted.

Every one of those songs contained an allusion to, or illusion of, motion. His characters were always driving cars trying to outrun Fate. I listened carefully to his lyrics, taking in every word like a particle of oxygen. I inhaled his songs; they resonated through my blood. The lyrics moved through me, the motion in beat with my heart.

He wrote these songs for me, his unknown muse. So what if he didn't realize that when he wrote them? How could he since he didn't even know I existed?

But then again, he did, in a way. I could have been any of the girls he wrote about: Wendy from "Born to Run," Mary from "Thunder Road," and my favorite, Terry from the passionate and mournful "Backstreets."

When he sang in his gravelly poet-voice, his trademark part snarl, part sob, "One soft infested summer, me and Terry became friends, trying in vain to breathe the fire we were born in" — I melted the same as those women did who, in their respective day, loved Sinatra or the Beatles. The line that got me most was, "But I hated him, and I hated you when you went away." What love! What passion! With all that hate, he could have been a Tingle.

His music painted a palpable throb of my personal teenage yearning. He created lyrical stories of people carrying on in spite of disappointments and never, ever giving up the hope of Getting Out.

And, like me, he came from a working-class family, disconnected from his parents, discontented with his tired little hometown. In fact, that a boy from Jersey could become such a huge success inspired me to follow my dream of becoming a writer.

Monica Priestly, my other best friend besides Tippi, went to St. Andrews, the private Episcopal school in town. She used to go to school with Tippi and me, but her father decided that Newitville Central was for morons and his daughter deserved better.

Monica was another hero of mine. She was witty beyond her years and made cuttingly clever remarks. We shared a love for clothes and fashion, investing as much of our parents' worth as we did our self-worth, into clothes. Monica's parents had way more money than mine—or than most people in Newitville. As a result of all that wonderful wealth, she dressed as stylishly as the models in *Vogue*. The local stores lack of the latest fashions didn't present a problem because her parents were divorced and her father lived in Dallas, hence, she shopped at Neiman Marcus and all the great stores of that big city.

Like me, she also read all the fashion magazines, plus *Rolling Stone*, where we learned that all rock stars shared one trait: they Got Out of their own private Newitville. Monica also wanted to Get Out. She aimed for a more exciting town like New York or LA — anything large and with a pulse and a spirit.

Monica had a raging curiosity — a trait not revered in Newitville. It made her "different" and being "different" was bad. For a young girl in Newitville, being different could mean anything from freaky to, in Monica's case, smart. Mrs. Priestly was different, too. She had a subscription to the Sunday *New York Times* and *French Vogue,* the latter being of more interest to me and Monica, though the only French words we knew were "Chanel," "Yves St. Laurent," and "bidet." A bidet became a symbol to us of the very rich and privileged, and Monica and I aspired to have bidet-lives when we were older.

Monica's father, Mr. Priestly was different, however. He was just damn rich. He owned a couple of different kinds of businesses, a true entrepreneur, and possessed the kind of wealth that characters in Bruce's songs dreamed about.

Monica's daddy also had hum-daddy looks. He lived in a north Dallas suburb with his second wife, a former catalogue model, and I knew that if the two of them ever got around to breeding, the resulting creature would be the object of desire for the masses. They both had chiseled features, matching verdant green eyes, her hair blonde, his the color of fine oak.

People in Newitville liked all that about Mr Priestly. He had made his money and got himself a pretty woman.

One of the things I liked best about Monica was that if I had plans with her during the weekend, she wouldn't ditch me if a cute guy asked her out. We became especially close our senior year because Tippi sort of exited the picture. She got a boyfriend and never had time for us. Monica had been that way when she had a boyfriend, but they broke up and now she dated different guys. She always made time for me, though.

Monica's heroic-index shot through the roof that year because of an extraordinary gift she gave me. She had spent Thanksgiving with her father and called me the Sunday she returned from Dallas. "Daddy gave us a little Christmas gift," she said, and I could tell she was squirming in her skin to contain her excitement. I knew it had to be good, but I didn't imagine this.

"Two tickets to see Bruce in Dallas in January. And he's even bought us the plane tickets."

I experienced a burst of elation that terminated abruptly when I thought of my parents. Plane and concert tickets were only a quarter of the battle to see Bruce. I needed their permission to go. I might as well perform brain surgery on myself right then and there; it would have been an easier feat.

"Monica, I'll call you back."

"Oh. Na-uh," Mama said when I told her and Daddy the news. It was happy hour. "We can't afford that. Hell!" Daddy said.

I had purposely approached them during happy hour, when they were lubricated. I knew that I could manipulate them easiest when they had a few cocktails in their system. So, to soften them up, I had cleaned their bathroom, as Mama never did (and certainly not Daddy).

The bathroom suffered from bourbon decay, so cleaning it had been no easy feat. I took a spray bottle of 409® and squirted half the contents onto the floors, walls, and porcelain. I let it sink in for a half-hour, then rolled up my sleeves, pulled on some rubber gloves, and armed myself with a mop and sponge. I don't know how they did it, but spilled bourbon was everywhere and soaked in, creating a gluey, sticky, part-sweet, part-rancid slime. It stuck to the window sill, in the tracks of the shower door, on the floor, on the back of the toilet. When I finished, the bathroom had this odd, almost shocked look, as if being clean were a foreign concept.

"Paying for Dallas isn't a problem," I said. "Mr. Priestly is treating."

Mama, who had just taken a sip of highball, sprayed it all over room, demonstrating to me how the bathroom had gotten so sticky to begin with.

"Good God Almighty! Have you hit your head or something? We can't let those people give us charity like that!"

"Fine. Then buy me a plane ticket and don't give me anything else for Christmas or my birthday."

"Na-uh. No ma'am. You're too young to be traveling without one of us." She jiggled her drink at me voodoo doll style. I was now cursed by Jack Daniel's.

"I'm not too young," I said. I was losing this battle and knew I needed a stronger defense than that.

"We can't let you run off to Dallas. Hell! Just you and Monica Priestly?" Daddy said.

"Na-uh!" Mama said, choking.

"But we're staying with her father and stepmother."

"Baby, they drink," Mama said in a low whisper.

"What do you call what are you doing right now?"

"That's different. We drink in private. They are public drinkers."

"Mama, you drove your truck through the Burger Chef because you were drunk."

"I was tired. I wasn't drunk." She gave a miffed look.

"Now that's in the past," Daddy said, wagging his finger a hair from my nose.

"People still talk about it, Daddy, and frankly, I will never forget it. So what if Mr. Priestly drinks a little? He never plowed his car through Burger Chef."

"Well." Mama said. There was a tortured moment of silence where we all ground our teeth. The room was alight with momentary and mutual hate: I was in the way of their having a peacefully drunken happy hour and they were KEEPING ME FROM SEEING BRUCE.

So I shifted my manipulation techniques into high gear.

I fell back against the bathroom wall and slid down till my butt rested on the floor. Then I put my head in my hands and pretended to sob. Uncontrollably.

"I have to go to Dallas," I whined. "I need to see the world."

"Hell, it's just Dallas!" Daddy said.

"It's what Dallas symbolizes."

"Symbolizes hell. Where did you learn that word? Don't tell me they are teaching you useless crap like that in school?"

"I guess. Isn't that where you learned it?"

He just shrugged and settled into himself, his face an overripe blueberry from anger. Then he muttered, "I can't remember that far back. Maybe I heard it on TV."

Mama felt the need to defend me. "She makes decent grades, Rodney. She learns things."

"I study hard," I whined. "All I do is study."

Now, this was so not true, but either they were having a sudden attack of politeness or they just didn't bother to correct me. I gave schoolwork just enough attention to get B's, except for Math, which I struggled with and felt relief whenever I made a C.

Mama said, "Doodie, we know you work hard. We all work hard."

I wiped my pretend tears and looked up. "Then you understand, so you should let me go see Bruce. I need this reward. I need to feel that all my hard work pays off."

"But it doesn't," Daddy said. "Hell, look at us. We can't afford to move out of this goddamn house. We've gotta live with those two crazy old coots."

"You don't think we want a reward?" Mama jiggled her drink at me again. "This is the reward, sugar. Jack Daniel's. That's the best we got."

If Bruce had been there, he would have been inspired to write another rock and roll opera like "Jungleland." I could almost hear him yowl, "In between these bathroom walls, Lisa cries out from the darkness of her grief. Mama is on her knees, Daddy just shakes his head. All they got is a fifth of Jack Daniel's and broken dreams."

"You can't go to Dallas," Mama said. "End of story."

"Period. Paragraph, Miss Symbolism," Daddy said.

I stood up. "I'm nearly eighteen. Pretty soon I will be making my own decisions. I am going to Dallas. Period. Paragraph. End of Story. Try to stop me."

I left the room, head high. I exited into their bedroom and slammed the bathroom door behind me.

Instantly, I heard Mama through the thin wood shriek, "Fuck!"

I froze. My brain screamed a silent "WHAT DID SHE SAY?"

To my knowledge Mama had never said "fuck." I didn't even think she knew the word existed.

"I am so sick of those motherfucking Priestlys," she said. "They control our daughter."

Motherfucking Priestlys? My mother knew things I thought people her age weren't allowed to know.

"Shuddup for God's sake, Belle," Daddy growled like a character straight from a Springsteen song.

"Our baby thinks more about those Priestly bastards than she does us."

"This ain't about the Priestlys. It's about that damn rock and roll hoodlum. She thinks she's in love."

After a pause, Mama asked. "You want another drink?"

"Hell yes."

The next morning at breakfast, Grandma put my oatmeal down in front of me. "So I hear you're running off to Dallas to see that hoodlum singer."

While nothing conclusive happened, other than my defiant declaration the previous night, I still said, "Yes 'um."

I looked up over my bowl at Mama and Daddy. Daddy's eyes were fixed on his coffee, Mama's on her OJ. I could tell she had been crying; her cheeks were splotchy, the area under her eyes puffy. It all meant one thing: I had won. I would be going to Dallas. I had dug in my heels and they would fight me no more.

From that day forward till the day I left for Dallas, we never spoke another word about Bruce or the Priestlys. Mama once referred to the concert as my "upcoming life-learning trip," and quickly changed the subject. Daddy didn't even bother to reference it at all.

The massive auditorium in Dallas was dark, save for the beam of white light in the center of the floor. Our seats were high in the stadium. "Close to heaven," Monica said, trying to make light of our distance from the stage.

The smell of pot permeated the air.

"Your grandma would be completely mortified if she knew we were around all these potheads." Monica clearly loved the fact that in Grandma's eyes we were being rebellious by virtue of simply being in the proximity of marijuana.

"It's exciting, isn't it?" I said, referring more to the moment than Grandma's mortification.

We had brought along Mr. Priestly's binoculars. They were affixed to my eyes. Bruce wore black jeans and a white t-shirt. He had come on stage wearing a leather jacket, but after a rousing "Rosalita," he tore it off and tossed it to the side near the giant amps, which sat like statues surrounding a cathedral. Bruce looked like a bohemian Jesus. He had dark curly hair and a bit of a beard, not quite a goatee. His eyes, I could see even with the binoculars, twinkled. He looked happy, enthusiastic. Comfortable. He was in his element.

Bruce took the full house prisoner, and it was good. We were happy to be captured. I sat among "my people," people who Got Bruce. In Newitville, only I loved him. Monica and Tippi tolerated him. Tippi was more into the

Commodores and Top 40, while Monica's Bruce was David Bowie.

As for the rest of Newitville, most people hadn't really heard much of his music — this was before his success of the eighties with "Born in the USA." WYRD in Jackson sometimes played the title track to *Born to Run*, which is how I first heard Bruce. I was in my room that day and when I heard that song, I sat still and listened to those lyrics. Music reached through my speakers and grabbed my soul by the throat. The words pierced my brain like an injection of lightning.

The concert did the same for me. It was part rock evangelism, and part downright fanatical-scary. A guy a few rows down from us was so moved by "Adam Raised a Cane," that he stood up and yelled, "You're God, man! You are God!"

When Bruce sang "Badlands," an anthem for many of his fans, every member of the crowd except for Monica shot their fist in the air on the refrain of the chorus. "Badlands, you gotta live it every day."

As my own fist shot in the air and Monica watched me with guarded, concerned eyes, I had an epiphany:

Mama and Daddy were characters from a Springsteen song. I loved his music because I thought he somehow wrote about me, and yet, he wrote about my parents, too. I was their car, a recurring theme in his songs as the vehicle of choice for exiting "a town full of losers" (to quote "Thunder Road").

The dream of Getting Out had been my car. Because of this music, I thought of Newitville as a place that "rips the bones from your back . . . a deathtrap, a suicide rap."

Through those songs, I understood clearly that I would not live and die in Newitville. Like Wendy in "Born to Run," I'd "get to that place where" I "really want to go." I just didn't know yet where that place would be, or what kind of symbolic or real car would take me there. But I knew if a scraggly Jersey boy could do it, why hell, it'd be a snap for a fashion conscious girl from Newitville, Mississippi.

A stadium of strangers, united as one gargantuan Bruce fan, danced in the rows. Except for Monica. She leaned over and whispered, "These people really are super crazy weird, you know."

"I know."

"I mean, this devotion to Bruce. It's really, well, kind of freaky. He's cute in a thug sort of way and all, but I don't know . . ."

Bless her, she just didn't get it. Probably because her parents weren't characters straight out of his songs. Sure, they had their issues, but nothing that called for yowling dark lyrics.

His next song was "The Night" and, embracing my epiphany, I decided this was a song strictly for Mama and Daddy. I thought of sending them a postcard from Dallas with the lines, "The world is busting at its seams, and you're just a prisoner of your dreams, holding on for your life."

But then Bruce launched into "Backstreets," with the lucky Terry from that "soft infested summer," and I forgot about my parents. I forgot that Grandpa, the cause of so much of my family's pain, was old and would die sooner rather than later and that it scared me and despite everything, I loved him and hated to see how his looming death worried Grandma, who herself was old and her life was winding down, too. Same with my parents. I had been their middle-age surprise, and by my own middle-age, chances are I would bury the two of them.

I forgot that I lived in a shabby, crowded house with four other people who made domestic war. I forgot that I was seventeen and really, really didn't know what would become of me.

I even forgot that I wanted to grow up and marry Bruce. And I forgot that the reason I loved Bruce to begin with was because of where he came from, a Northern version of my life. And that what he had accomplished meant I could Get Out; I could succeed at something, too. In fact, as I sat there, I didn't think about anything. There was just the music. That's all that mattered. Twenty years later and looking back, the music was all I ever really needed from Bruce. His songs reaffirmed the notion that maybe I was born to run, or at least born to Get Out of Newitville.

Chapter Eight
All or Nothing at All

How did my family get to be the way they were? I knew most of the stories about their past, I just somehow couldn't connect the dots and figure out why it all came to be as it had. If I could do this, I reasoned, I could help this family get right in the head.

I suspected their problems started before Daddy and Mama even met. My parents were bitter about a lot of things, and I had an idea about when the bitterness started.

Their hearts were broken and they were broken by each other. My parents wanted what I wanted all along: to Get Out of Newitville. But they stayed, and they each kept the other back. The result was a chain reaction throughout my family.

This idea of fixing my family came to me late in my senior year of high school as I spent much time seriously pondering what was wrong with my family. I wanted to fix them before I moved on because I knew deep in my bones, down to the marrow, down to the first atom of my life, that I would Get Out.

To fix them, I had to figure out where and when things started to go wrong. I thought about my very first ever memory, and knew that had all the clues. I have a mental picture of myself as a child waving to my father as he drove off in our 1967 Plymouth Valiant. He would return later that night, long after I had gone to bed and was well into dreams of eating Sugar Babies and getting licked on the ear by Dino Martin, my dog.

Daddy was going to the northern part of Mississippi to watch the Ole Miss Rebels whup the Mississippi State Bulldogs in the state's most important football game. As he backed down the gravel driveway, rocks crunching under the car wheels, he yelled out the window, "Go Rebs!" to which I yelled back with my fist raised high in the air, "Whoop them *dawgs*!"

Mama and I stood at the top of the driveway, watching until the taillights disappeared down our winding road and we could no longer hear the Valiant's engine. Mama took my hand and looked lovingly into my eyes.

And this is it, these are the words I have retained in my memory as the ones I first remember Mama saying to me:

"Sugar, you want to watch your crazy mama get drunk?"

We walked hand-in-hand to my parents' lime green, faux marble, Caesar's Palace-wannabe bathroom. I dug my Scarlett O'Hara Barbie out of the bathroom linen closet, where I had played with it the night before, and the night before that though my memory doesn't extend any farther back.

I remember flopping Barbie around as Mama mixed a cocktail. I pulled at the doll's hair and lifted one leg to peer at her blank anatomy.

Mama sat on her black vinyl barstool and sipped her cocktail while a Sinatra album played "All or Nothing at All." I squeezed Barbie's head off and held her thick mane between my fingers, then thumped her face against the door of the linen closet. The spooky cadence reminded me of a story Ava tortured me with. It was about a headless man who rode his horse through the black night scaring Pilgrims half out of their minds.

"Lisa, sugar, tonight I'm going to share something about your daddy, something you don't know. That man loved me so much he lied his butt off so I'd marry him. I wasn't too smart. He looked good and I fell for him and his lie like a damned fool." Then she giggled like Ava did over a cute boy.

She jiggled her drink at me. "Sugar, the past is the most powerful thing in the world. It's all there is. No present, no future. It's all the past. You'll know what I mean one day, just watch."

I pressed Barbie's cheeks imagining I could squirt brains out of her ears. I stared into her vacant blue eyes. She looked back at me and in my memory, which I know is false,

I see her saying, "It's all there is, sugar," in my mother's voice.

"When I met your daddy, I had one of those bobby-soxer crushes on Frank Sinatra."

She went on to tell me that as much as she had this fantasy about leaving Newitville and marrying Sinatra, she understood the implausibility of it. My mother looked around the farm where she grew up, saw all the cows, chickens, and her own mother's weathered face, and knew that kind of life could easily be her own one day.

Then Daddy came along and made her feel special. Plus he threw in something extra to seal the deal.

"He told me he had come from money, and more so, that he had every intention to make his own fortune. I should have listened carefully to his words, Lisa, because the key word was 'had.' He *had* come from money. Long ago, his family lost every cent in the depression. But he didn't tell me that till after we were married a month later. I know it's insane to marry so quickly and don't you ever get any ideas like that when you grow up."

"Were you mad when you found out?" I asked.

"Hell yes. But he calmed me down. I was in love, I guess, and I also had hope. His hopes. He really thought he would make a fortune."

Specifically, Daddy planned to own a chain of appliance stores. He envisioned a fleet of shiny washers, dryers, stoves, and refrigerators. A team in suits would pitch the wares' virtues to customers, while another team of men in neat blue shirts and matching pants with soda jerk hats would arrive at customers' homes with tool boxes and pearly smiles to fix broken Whirlpools. And after meeting Mama at the USO dance where she sang Sinatra tunes, he wanted her to sing the radio jingle to the tune of "All or Nothing at All."

"*Tingle One Stop Appliance . . . We sell them and we fix them, too.*" At the end, she would purr, "*You need a Tingle.*"

Mama could relate to a man with vision, particularly a vision that involved her singing, and she fell for Daddy, pushing aside her crush for Sinatra. Granted, the appliance world did not sound glamorous, but she reasoned that for a life of security, she could let go of her unrequited love for

Sinatra. Her own mother, a meticulous hard worker with a solid dictum for all of life's situations, had no glossy dreams. Yet she was loved, admired and respected by everyone in Newitville. Her husband adored her. He watched her simplest moves, laughed at her smallest jokes, and took to heart even the most prosaic of her advice. Mama wanted a man who would adore her that way. You could call it a backup dream.

"But a year passed and we were struggling to get by. Your daddy had a job at Dixie Refrigeration repairing air-conditioners. I worked as an operator at the phone company. I'll be honest with you. I started thinking about Frank again. I started thinking how glamorous a divorce sounded and how I would leave your father and just run off to Hollywood. Your daddy could tell he was losing me. So you know what he did? He found out Frank Sinatra was coming nearby, down in New Orleans. He bought me a ticket to the show."

At first, Mama said no. She told him the gesture was sweet, but that they couldn't afford the gas for the four hour car trip. She'd save the ticket in her jewelry box, which was really just an old cigar box.

But she thought about that ticket every second. A clock in her head wound down to the day Sinatra performed. She couldn't go. The ticket was a test, given to her not only by Daddy, but also by Fate or God or Frank Sinatra — whoever was pulling the strings of the universe. She had made her bed by marrying Rodney Tingle, now she would lie in it. She had to let go of her silly-girl dreams once and for all.

The ticket glowed inside the box, however. Only she could see its light. She knew she had to give her fantasy life one last shot, and she had to do it alone.

"So I took our car early one morning and left your daddy a note on the kitchen table, saying, 'I'm going to see Frank. I know you don't understand, but this is something I need to do — alone. Besides, you still owe me for that lie you told. P.S. There's some leftover spaghetti in the refrigerator. P.P.S. Thank you again for the ticket. It was really sweet.' I didn't want to make him feel too bad, you know."

When Daddy found out she had left, he went after her in a borrowed Christmas green truck with "Rebel Plumbing" written on the side in red. Though it was a four-hour drive, he found Mama almost right away. She was standing in a thicket of women outside the Saenger Theatre, waiting to be let inside for the performance. He weaved his way into the tangle, yelling to anyone who crossed him, "Move, damnit, I'm here to get my wife."

Daddy finally reached Mama and tugged on her arm. "Belle, are you crazy? Driving down here by yourself like a fool? I told you I'd take you."

"His timing could not have been worse, Lisa. Right then, the doors to the theater opened and the swell of women surged forward. I broke free. 'I need to do this alone, Rodney' I said, looking back at him. 'Besides, I'm still mad that you lied. I know you've tried to make amends, but you told a big lie, Rodney Tingle, a very big lie.'

"'Damn woman! I love you! Doesn't that count for something? Frank Sinatra doesn't even know who the hell you are!'

"Lisa, I just slit my eyes all mean, and without a word, turned forward, letting the flow of the crowd ease me inside. Your father stood back, allowing the female swarm to flow past him into the theater. He had come all this way, but he knew there was no point, he had to let me live out the fantasy.

"I ended up on the third row, center stage. The auditorium was full of females, screaming, crying, holding up their hands and swaying, as if trying to get closer to their love or trying to feel the spirit of our blue-eyed hero. I was so close I could see the scar on Sinatra's cheek from where a doctor's forceps had squeezed him during his breached birth.

"I wanted to reach past the women in the first two rows and touch that scar. I really wanted to know what imperfection on the face of perfection felt like. That scar meant not only that he had flaws, but that his life had its troubles, and if he had troubles, then everyone did, not just me and your daddy.

"Sinatra's voice, velvet sliding across air, wooed me. I lifted my hand so I could grab an invisible note, then I held it close to my heart, hoping it would absorb through my pores and fill me with Frank.

"During 'All or Nothing at All,' he took off his bow tie and threw it to the screaming audience. I reached up and it landed in my outstretched palms, as if Frank had meant for me to catch it. He winked, then moved down the stage.

"I smelled the tie, inhaling Frank's touch. Suddenly, running off to New Orleans and leaving my husband didn't seem so foolish. I was living my destiny, Lisa. And then, a girl from behind me snatched the tie right out of my hand. I lunged for her, but she climbed over her seat and scampered away."

Mama stopped at this point and looked at me. "That little bitch. I could have gone after her but I couldn't bare leaving my seat so close to Frank. After the performance, I waited at the stage door. I wasn't alone. A crowd of girls gathered. Frank finally came out, surrounded by the New Orleans police who squeezed him through the crowd.

"'Frank, Frank!' I screamed, but he looked straight ahead. He passed right by me, so close that I could smell the cigarette odor of his coat. Sinatra kept his eyes focused ahead. He didn't even look at me.

"I looked around at all the women popping in their heels like jumping beans, screaming, crying, sweating over a man who did not even know they existed. And right then, I thought of Rodney. He liked Sinatra's music simply because I did. And he had wasted no time getting to New Orleans to bring me home, which was so sweet and romantic.

"I knew then life with Rodney would be ordinary, but maybe that was my destiny. I thought, 'There's nothing wrong with ordinary, after all.' So I pushed my way through the girls and ran out onto Canal Street. I wanted to find your daddy, throw my arms around him and beg his forgiveness. I had been a fool, chasing a big star, a married man.

"But Rodney wasn't there. I sat down on the street curb and started to cry because I had just lost a future with someone who loved me. A real man, not a fantasy.

"The lights of the Saenger marquee buzzed over my head. Sinatra's name lit up the darkening sky. At the far end of the street, where it dead-ended into the Mississippi River, heavy weather rolled in. I didn't care if the rain came and drenched me. I covered my face with my hands and cried.

"After a while, I felt a hand on my shoulder. It was Rodney.

"He squatted down and handed me a piece of paper. It was a dinner tab from the Acme Oyster bar. It read, 'One Po-Boy and three Dixie Beers.'

"'Other side,' he said. 'I wrote it while I was eating.'

"I flipped the bill over and saw a poem in his handwriting.

'I love you
And you love Frank
My brain feels damaged
I have only myself to thank
I told a lie
You ran away
Without you in my life
I can't live another day.'"

Mama looked at me when she finished reciting the poem. "And I woke up the next morning and Frank Sinatra was out of my system. Crush over. End of story."

I thought about this story and the night Mama told it to me quite a lot the last semester of my senior year. Maybe it was because I was getting nostalgic: I would soon go off to college, albeit, just to Millsaps over in Jackson, 45 miles to the East. Or maybe I saw parallels between Mama and me, my desire to get away versus my desire to marry my own version of Sinatra, Springsteen, another Jersey boy.

What I do know is I spent a lot of time lying on my bed, listening to records and thinking of this story and many others that my family told repeatedly throughout my life. Small stories that were insignificant but I pondered them like they held hidden keys to the mysteries of my family. Like how they named me Lisa after Judy Garland's daughter Liza. Grandma thought Liza sounded trampy, so they settled on the more common Lisa. Ava Gardner Tingle was named after the actress, Frank Sinatra's greatest love. Grandma thought Ava sounded like a person with potential, so my parents didn't have to compromise on her name.

Then there was the story about how Daddy didn't have the money to buy the appliance store he had dreamed of, but within a few years they had saved enough to open a small air-conditioning retail and repair business. It looked like they would do okay. Mama never sang the Tingle jingle, though. Radio ads cost too much.

For a while, they entertained Daddy's buddies and customers at weekly cocktail parties. Mama sang for their social circle in the living room of her and Daddy's small apartment in downtown Newitville, and in a way she had a Newitville-scaled version of the Hollywood life she wanted. Everyone considered her one of the prettier "gals" of their bunch. She liked Daddy's buddies and she liked the attention they gave her.

One by one, all their friends had children and the social circle drifted apart. Mama and Daddy worked harder to make more money, not only because the family had grown with the birth of Ava, but so had the competition for business. They couldn't make it, and not too long after I came along, they declared bankruptcy.

Of course, where the stories ended the drinking began. Rather than get mad at my father for his failing business, she would have a highball or two, or three each night.

Other than recalling stories from their past, I never heard Mama and Daddy talk much during Happy Hour, except to complain about the way my grandparents' judged them for drinking. In my efforts to entertain as a kid, I would sometimes swoop in, caught up in a game where I was a tap dancer in Vegas. I would fling my arms, jerk my head back and forth and rap-a-tap-tap my feet. My parents would smile at my performance and clap. On my way out, I'd notice that Mama and Daddy would resume what they had been doing before my intrusion: they would take a swig of their drink, listen quietly to the music, and stare at the tub, just trying to make the best of things.

Chapter Nine
Reunion

There was not an exact moment when I decided to move away from my family. The thought of Getting Out popped up everyday throughout the years: every time Mama drank or my parents and grandparents fought.

Ava must have had the thought, too, because she found the answer by marrying several times. We never discussed it, but I understood what she was doing. And I knew I had to have a better method as hers only ended up in a different version of our family.

Somehow, all the experiences crystallized in my mind. I had to leave, get far away, get a good job, a career. And no matter what I did, at all costs, I had to stay away from Jack Daniel's. And if I married, I had to keep my in-laws where they belonged, which would not be under my roof.

Perhaps my friends, Monica and Tippi deserve some credit for this passion. We would talk of Growing Up and Getting Out in junior high and throughout high school. In fact, Getting Out became as important a rite of passage as Graduation and College. It ranked with Getting Married and Getting Rich; maybe higher. We knew that Getting Out would be the most important thing we ever did; we believed our lives would not begin until that day.

Some kids grow up fantasizing about husbands and nice homes and kids. Tippi Blunt did. She married at nineteen to a boy she met during her freshman year at the University of Southern Mississippi. She got pregnant and dropped out of school. Not that she had ever intended to graduate. Her idea of Getting Out was simply to leave Newitville and move to a major southern city, nothing too far from home, but far enough away that she could redefine herself.

"I want to go to a place where there are at least three shopping malls," she told me once. "You're not in a big town till you have at least three malls." She'd read somewhere that a city should have a mall for every 100,000 people. So 300,000 sounded big enough to her — it was bigger (at the time) than Jackson, the state capital.

The newlyweds moved to Charleston, where the groom took a job at his uncle's country club as assistant manager. Every now and then I'd get a postcard from her, something with an Old South theme, talking at first about her baby then her next pregnancy, and then of being a mother of two. The only clue I ever had as to how she really felt about her life was from one postcard of Ft. Sumter I received during my junior year of college. On the back, she wrote, "Charleston's just big enough where I know the right people, but everyone doesn't know me."

Monica and I had different dreams than Tippi. We wanted jet-set schedules and overstuffed address books filled with our best friends — successful bon vivants, authors, artists, musicians.

We fantasized about moving to New York. I would be a journalist, she would be an actress. We would fly all over the world and socialize with famous people. Champagne would be part of our daily diet. We would blow our money on clothes.

It sounds shallow now, but really, we thought we only had two choices. We could either live in Newitville, or the larger and smaller variations of it like Jackson or McGee. Or we could be part of the high-living world we read about. The closest we came to that life, though, was Mr. Priestly. Whenever Monica returned from visiting him in Dallas, she brought back stories that were kind of like something out of *People* magazine. Mr. Priestly didn't exactly know stars or fascinating artists, but he knew Dallas society, some of whom knew stars or fascinating artists. He ran with the edges of the society that fringed the gamut of the jet set. We lived vicariously through that.

Even as teenagers, we understood that life was short; we could either let our souls and spirits rot in a town like Newitville or we could, well, hang with the overly accomplished. We didn't consider the quiet existence, that in-between zone of life not desperate but not frenetic with glamour. We didn't consider it because we didn't know anyone who lived in it.

After high school we both went to Millsaps College in Jackson, a small liberal arts school that was the best in the state. I majored in English Literature because they didn't have a journalism program, and spent my free time working for the school paper. Monica majored in theater.

She clocked in a year and quit. Life would not begin she reasoned till she Got Out of Mississippi. She moved to San Francisco, because it was cutting edge and New York was over. She took a job at a record store, but that didn't last long. Her father hated seeing his smart, talented daughter work for minimum wage, so he asked her what she really wanted to do. Her dream of acting had given way to the record business. She wanted her own independent label. Mr. Priestly gave her a little seed money, and she shrewdly managed it. Soon she was signing young post-punk bands from all over the Bay Area.

Monica called her new endeavor Audacious Records, which seemed fitting, because she had audacity in spades.

I, however, lacked her boldness. I stayed in Mississippi and finished college. I liked Jackson. I had friends that were writers and thespians.

My two closest new friends were Kate and Charlie. Kate was a tall, rich blonde who grew up in an antebellum home in the Delta. She had runway model looks and once dated a man from New York, who we were convinced was in the Mafia. She always dated on-the-edge type of guys. Then there was Charlie, a gay guy from Biloxi with the exotic features of his Lebanese ancestry. He could do everything: cook like someone gifted by Mt. Olympus, sing, dance, act, even cut hair.

Like me, Kate and Charlie read Eudora Welty, Walker Percy, and Tennessee Williams. They also listened to good music, everything from Springsteen to newer stuff (for the times) like Gang of Four. And like me, they wanted to Get Out. Yet they showed me a twist to that wish. These friends taught me to appreciate the fact that Mississippi was the one state in the union that gave the world not only James

Meredith, but also Robert Johnson, Elvis and of course, *of course*, Faulkner.

My friends had such hope and dreams and intelligence that they managed to make me feel it was possible that one far away day some awestruck college kid at Millsaps would think of the state as the place that gave the world Ms. Lisa Tingle.

After graduation, I started working as a reporter for an alternative paper in Jackson. I liked my job. I liked my friends. I think it's fair to say that I even liked my life. So I might still be in Jackson if it weren't for what happened a few months after graduation.

Grandpa died.

And it was my old friends who reentered my life and changed things. Monica and Tippi returned to Newitville for the funeral.

Tippi used the trip home as an excuse to ditch her kids and spend some time catching up with old friends. Without Monica and Tippi, the funeral would have been a lot worse. They provided a barrier between me and my overwrought mother. I have only one memory of Mama that night. She sat in a chair against the wall at the funeral home, her face swollen, her eyes red. In my memory, a handkerchief is semi-attached to her nose. She didn't talk to anyone. But she grieved hard and proper, crying a tear for every bad and maybe good feeling she ever had about her father.

Grandma cried, too. Loud, constant almost. "I miss my old sweetheart," she kept saying. "I'm ready to lay my old bones down and die. Lord take me now!"

It sounds melodramatic. It was, and somehow it was funny. At least Monica, Tippi and I laughed a little.

Cousin Van came, as mean as ever. He'd left Newitville five years earlier after a fight with his mother, my Aunt Teckla. No one knew what had happened, or no one would tell me.

Van brought his girlfriend with him, a stripper from Mobile, where they both lived.

"I'm Big Red," she said, walking up to people and shaking their hand. To everyone, even non-family, even mere family acquaintances, she would express her sympathy. "I'm so sorry for your loss, sugar. Death is so hard on everyone."

"Not to me, not this death!" Daddy declared. He was the only cheery person there. He did act a bit lost, though, staying away from Mama and Grandma, who were emoting way beyond his comfort level, and not spending too much time talking to anyone lest they bring up his poor relationship with Grandpa and questioned his attendance. He was there for Mama, pure and simple. He'd much rather have been at the VFW pounding back a few JD's with his war buddies.

Van was slightly more appropriately behaved than my father. He hugged Grandma, kissed her on the cheek, then walked up to Grandpa's casket and stared at him for a few moments. Then he motioned to Big Red and they walked out. He hadn't even said a word to Aunt Teckla. She watched him as he left. She had her arm around Grandma, who was wailing over not only Grandpa's death, but the momentary return of her prodigal grandson.

Delia, my other cousin, was there. She was a missionary for the Church of Jesus Christ Our Savior. She wore a dark blue suit with a skirt that fell to the middle of her calves. The bun in her hair was pulled so tight it gave her face a semi-lift.

She said "Praise the Lord" a lot and was a cheerful Christian who laughed at most jokes, even the off-color ones and especially the racist ones. She even giggled when, after asking Daddy, "Have you asked God to forgive you for the hatred you and Grandpa held toward each other," he replied "That old bastard is probably burning in hell right now."

"Our grandpa's home now," Delia said to me after Daddy excused himself to go to the men's room. I felt cornered, being left alone with her. I had an irrational fear she would ask me if I'd been saved, or want me to talk about God. I found God a difficult subject to talk about. So many Southerners can do it joyously. Perhaps, as an act of rebellion at a young age, I distanced myself from the big G and never made my way back. He was more a character in fiction to me, the protagonist of the Bible, than a personal savior. Or was Jesus supposed to be my personal savior? I couldn't get even the basics of Christianity straight.

"Grandpa's with the good Lord above," Delia said, almost singing. "He's at peace! Praise God!"

I excused myself, only to run into Ava who had just arrived. She had a new boyfriend, Bobby. He hadn't met any of the family until today.

He stuck his hand out. "Hey little Sis. Hell of a time to meet, huh?"

His skin felt smooth, cool, a bit slick. I thought of a peeled boiled egg. I would later learn that Bobby's god-given name had been Wolf. He got tired of the jokes and changed it to Bobby, short for Robert, short for Robert E. Lee, his hero.

Lucy and JW, my niece and nephew, were in tow. I had probably seen them three times in their lives, mainly because that's how many often Ava had come back to Newitville to see the family. Lucy was about six going on fifteen. She had a large vocabulary and knew words like "sex," as a verb, and phrases like "drug use." As in "Mama's best friend Debbie has a problem with drug use and she is addicted to sex as well."

JW, named after John Wayne (whom Ava considered the greatest American), was four and had a more limited vocabulary befitting someone his age. He liked to say the word, "fork," an awful lot. It was his answer for anything.

"How are you, JW,"
"Fork."
"Did you finish your homework, JW?"
"Fork."

Both children were products of her third marriage, which, according to the divorce papers ended for "irreconcilable differences."

Truthfully, her husband was a Peeping Tom nicknamed Shakey. Ava left Shakey because he got arrested too many times and it just got too embarrassing even for her. He now lived in Parchment, the state prison.

Ava wore a new engagement ring; a tiny sliver of a diamond. Wolf/Bobby might become husband number four, though she'd been engaged before and the relationship hadn't ended in marriage. Daddy and I called all her ex loves, "Ava's souvenirs."

"Oh hey," Ava said. "This is kind of sad, huh?"

She had blue lines stacking up under her eyes. She was still painfully thin, and her skin had a pallor that beat all the other pallor ghosting her face over the years. And her voice sludged as if enthusiasm were unattainable. She lived in Alabama now, right across the Mississippi line. Wolf/Bobby was a postal worker. Ava worked as a secretary in an auto parts shop. I hadn't talked to her since Christmas three years earlier. She had moved out of our house by the time I was eight, and we were never sisterly-close.

I always felt a bond with her, though, formed from living on the outside of a bottle of Jack Daniel's and constantly looking in. Also, I also felt gratitude toward Ava. As the first born, she suffered the full assault of Mama and Daddy's target practice as parents.

"You look tired, Ava," I said. "Are you sleeping?"

"Oh yeah, sure. It's just. Well. Kids. They are the surest way to age beyond your years."

"Yeah?"

"Uh-huh. So didn't you graduate from college recently?"

"Yeah, I did."

"Oh. Great. Good for you. Got plans?"

"Yeah, lots of plans."

"How about that," she looked past me and became animated. "JW, put that God-damned flower down! That's Grandpa's wreath, for Pete's sake!"

And then she was off, chasing after JW, who had decided to eat flowers from the many wreaths surrounding the coffin.

My niece Lucy, on the other hand, had discovered Monica and was asking her questions about boys and makeup. Monica looked trapped talking to the child, as if she had been accosted by a large rodent. I thought of saving her when Tippi walked up and stopped me.

"That look on Monica's face is priceless."

"I think she may need therapy after this," I said. I didn't want to hurt Tippi's feelings, since she had kids, but Monica's distaste outsized even mine.

"Children are the product of pedestrian dreams," she would say. "They're overrated. What's wrong with people?

Can't they use their creativity for art instead of breeding?" She really meant these things she said, which made her endearing to most people. She was like a sober version of someone in my family, saying things your average Joe just wouldn't even conceive of. Like Mama's deeply held belief that television was a great educational tool. And in an odd way, she was right. TV helped teach me about life beyond the shaggy corners of Newitville.

"So how's life?" I asked Tippi.

"Really, really, *really* great." She had a tight smile on her face. I stared at her and didn't say a word. I had learned in the only journalism class taught at Millsaps that when a reporter wants his subject to reveal more, he shuts up.

"I mean, you know, I get tired chasing after the kids, especially that little Amy." She's two now and just so full of . . . I don't know. Energy. You're mad at me for getting married and doing all this."

"Ugh," I responded, caught off guard. I hadn't really intended for our small talk to turn into a confrontation.

"I don't want to take away from your grandfather's day, you know, I really don't. But I just have to get this off my chest. You make me feel like I betrayed you by making the choices I've made. And I'm sorry. I know we talked about doing all these fantastic things with our life, but I like my life. I do. It's not perfect. It's not glamorous, that's for sure. But it's sweet. It's just fast enough, or maybe it's just slow enough."

I didn't say anything, this time it wasn't a journalist's trick; I just didn't know how to respond — to anything, to her confrontation, to my grandfather's death. I had only my family as examples of how to react, and given their history, they didn't seem like the best role models.

But Tippi let me off the hook by talking more. "So I miss going out at night," Then she turned red and almost started to cry. "I mean, I love my life, and I wouldn't trade it for the world, but sometimes I think about us when we were in high school. We had some fun, you know."

"I know."

And then it happened. I started to feel again. There were two words that summed up how I felt: damn bad. I felt bad about Grandpa and I felt bad about the way I treated

Tippi. I felt bad for not being closer to my family. Except for Van. He didn't deserve my guilt, the jackass.

"I'm sorry, Tippi," I said. I got teary-eyed and mad. I was teary-eyed for the ass-whooping Grandpa's death did to my heart and soul and mad because there was nothing I hated more than crying in public, even at a funeral. Grandpa never cried, especially in public. Hell, he wouldn't have broken down over the triple death of a puppy, a kitten and a sparky toddler dying simultaneously of leukemia.

"For what?" she asked, as if we hadn't just had this conversation.

"I never call you; I only write when you write to me first. I mean, you committed no crime other than wanting different things than me."

"No. I'm sorry. I'm talking about me and my feelings when you just lost your grandfather. I'm really sorry about him, you know, dying," Tippi said. "He was as crazy as a road lizard."

"Grandpa was crazy all right," I said to Tippi. "We're a crazy family, though."

"There's lots of anger in your family, that's for sure. Like, why didn't your grandpa and your daddy speak?" she asked.

"Oh Tippi," I said, "I barely understand that myself, much less any other mysteries of the universe."

Tippi had asked The Question, and I knew it was the missing component in why I felt so numb about Grandpa's death. I found Daddy, who seemed to be hiding behind a wreath.

"What are you doing?"

"Smelling flowers," he said, sounding defensive.

"Why didn't you and Grandpa talk?"

"We communicated."

"Why didn't you speak to each other?"

"I said, we communicated."

"But you didn't talk. Why did you communicate without words?"

"It's a long story. I want to go home. Tell your mother I'll be outside when she's ready to go."

I found Ava, who was swatting JW on the behind and telling him that it was wrong to steal. I didn't pry; I really didn't want to know.

"Ava, why didn't Daddy and Grandpa speak?" I asked her.

She looked at me like I had just asked the most thought provoking question ever uttered.

"Well . . . you know . . . I just got so used to them not talking I never questioned why."

Ava's answer summed up why I never pressed the subject of Daddy and Grandpa's feud. I had been raised with people who didn't speak. It was the norm. I ignored it.

I cornered Bitty, my mother's first cousin. She had driven up from New Orleans. Bitty was a gossip, the family grapevine. She knew everything, or at least had a version of her own brand of the truth.

"Why didn't they speak?" She repeated my question as she ran a wrinkled, manicured hand through her short brown hair. "Well, your grandfather didn't like your father. He thought he lacked merit and all since he had lied to your mother. Do you know that when they met, he told her that he had money?"

"I know. I know." Mama has told me a million times. She and Daddy met at a USO dance, and Daddy told her he came from major money. He didn't lie, he just neglected to say that they had lost every penny during the Depression. The story she told was that he "fibbed" because he was so smitten with her.

"So anyway, over the years, it just irked your grandfather that your mother would marry a liar. No offense toward your daddy. You know how your grandfather could get all dramatic."

"I guess."

"Your mother chose your father's love over your grandfather's respect. Hence, all the trouble!" She held her hands out like she had just given me a prize. Then she said, in a low, confidential tone. "You know, Teckla and Pie almost barred your mother and father from the funeral!"

"What?"

She nodded, her red lipsticked lips pursed in the glory of knowledge. "Oh yes, they said she has acted so abhorrently against your old grandpa over the years, and what with your father not talking to him and vice versa. Well, they relented in the end for your sake."

"How kind," I said, stunned. Pie and Teckla really thought it was their place, their privilege to keep their own sister from her father's funeral? The family gene that rendered Hate ran deep and far.

"Oh there's Ava. You know, that girl looks ill. I wonder if she's doing drugs?" the thought nearly drove Bitty mad with delight; her eyes were practically doing loops in her head.

Next I asked cousin Carson, my overly romantic cousin who now lived in Baton Rouge where she taught Yoga. Carson had grown into the type of woman that kept sentimental Hallmark cards in production. She dressed in flowing dresses with much with a lot of lace. She quoted Elizabeth Browning frequently and read a lot of poetry, finding prose too plain.

"You look simply devastated," she said.

"I feel sad," I said. Then I corrected myself because that wasn't accurate. "I feel empty."

"That's the feeling of eternal loss," she told me casually. "You'll grow accustomed to it, I'm afraid to say. We are all going to die and the feeling of utter loss will return with each and every death, pricking your heart, bleeding your soul dry."

She truly talked this way, like every word was the draft of a bad poem forming in her head. I often wondered if she had delusions of a spotlight constantly on her, that she existed for an unseen audience.

I told her about my conversation with Bitty, how Teckla and Pie didn't want Mama to come.

"Adults behaving badly," Carson said, shaking her head with distaste.

And then I told her what Bitty had said about the reason my father and grandfather didn't talk.

"Why that's simply not true!" Carson put a hand over her heart. "Don't you know?"

"Know what?"

"The truth!"

I shook my head.

"Well, it's not surprising I suppose. See, if you could walk over to that coffin and shake Grandpa back into existence, he himself couldn't tell you why he and Uncle Rodney stopped talking. It was so long ago and there were so many little fights over silly things like who built the house, who owned it, and who was entitled to this electric bill rebate and who owed that whatever bill . . . well, it just got easier to not talk."

"That's it?"

"Well, that's a lot. It wasn't just one event. Sugar, nothing is ever one event. That's fiction. Reality is always more complicated, and sometimes, a little more dull." She paused. "It's the same with Teckla and Van, you know. Years of fighting, then one day –" she made a motion with her hands of breaking an invisible twig in two.

Before I could ask Carson any more questions, she felt compelled to go save Ava from Bitty. "Bitty is insane, you know. She has a Louella Parsons complex. She feels she is in-the-know about everything. Very strange bird, that woman."

She left me and I stood alone. I looked around the room. All the most familiar faces in the world to me were here. I saw Grandma, crying, undone, bewildered and feeling alone for the first time. Mama still sat in the corner, a child reprimanded for the rest of her life for disobeying her father. She was quiet, a wallflower with a soaked white handkerchief attached to her hand. There was Daddy, cowering behind the wreath. He didn't belong here and no one knew it better than he did. Teckla and Pie acted as hostesses, but I knew they were wounded, they loved Grandpa. Somehow, they escaped his judgment.

Ava and Tippy huddled together now, worn from marriage and children and wondering how they ended up with a permanent case of melted makeup and sore feet.

Seeing them made me wonder how I looked to my family and my friends. What did Monica think of the person I had become? I feared she saw me as trapped, pedestrian, embracing mediocrity and not even knowing it. She stood tall by a large reef as she herself surveyed the room, her eyes missing mine. Her chin was jetted, her eyes engaged as if in conversation. She had a slight smile on her face and I recognized it. She was happy that this was just a visit. She loved her new life. Her happiness mocked us all.

As I was watching her, she turned her focus on me. She slowly waved a finger, beckoning me. I walked over to her.

"So tell me something," she said, and paused like she was hearing a drum roll in her head, waiting for the proper moment of heightened effect. "Are you ready to finally Get Out?"

Chapter Ten
Getting Out is Hard to Do

After the funeral, I knew I would soon leave Mississippi. I had waited for this moment my whole life. Getting out of Newitville wasn't enough. Moving to Jackson wasn't Getting Out. It was just getting a little distance between me and my family.

At the funeral, Monica said. "You look like your feeling defeated."

"Grandpa is dead," I said. I tried to cover my feelings. But she was in Jesus-mode, all knowing, a great seer of truth and prophecy. And dead-on.

"It's more than that. You have always wanted to move away and here you are."

"Here I am."

"Move to San Francisco," she commanded in her Monica way. "You might as well commit suicide if you live anywhere else."

And that did it, that simple proclamation that life was not worth living outside of San Francisco was my kick in the ass.

"Okay," I said. "Okay, damnit."

I could not Get Out though, so soon after Grandpa died. Grandma was a different woman now. She was less overpowering. She talked often of her "old sweetheart" and said she was ready to lay her "old bones down and die" if only God would take her.

Grandma was weak, something she had never been.

So I told Monica, whom I would live with in San Francisco, that I would have to stay in Jackson for six more months. I would save some money and, in the meantime, console Grandma as best as I could. I worked days at my newspaper job, and for extra income, took a night job at the Ramada Inn working as a bartender for special events.

I did not grieve like a normal person would about Grandpa. I never cried, apart from that single tear I shed on the day he died. This remained true for five years. Then I shed one tear: It was the middle of the day and I had a familiar memory, of Grandpa taking me to get ice cream at the Dairy Queen. I pictured his hair sticking up the way it always did like gray flames, and I saw him licking the cone piled high with vanilla. After I wiped away that tear, I went out and got an ice cream cone. Chocolate. I always had chocolate, he always had vanilla.

I never told my family of my plans to move. Though I hinted at it once.

"One day, I might go to grad school in San Francisco," I said at a Sunday dinner in the late summer after Grandpa had died.

"Wait till we're dead," Daddy said. "We couldn't stand having our baby leave."

"Oh God that would be awful," Mama said.

"I couldn't bear it," Grandma agreed.

"It's just a thought. I mean, I have to do something with my life."

"You're doing all right," Daddy said.

"Good enough," Mama said.

"Pass the butter-beans," Grandma said.

And I never brought it up again.

The holidays came. I reasoned that I could not leave my family during Christmas: losing me right after Grandpa would be too much for them. Still, I went to the library and researched Bay Area colleges. I finally applied to San Francisco State University for a masters in Creative Writing. I sent the application to Monica, who put it in a different envelope and sent it from her address. I had started having mail sent to her house to establish California residency.

February came, and I thought, "I can't leave near Valentine's Day." Then there was Easter. I almost let that holiday pass for the same reasons as before, but then I thought of the significance of Easter, it was the day Jesus rose from the dead. I liked the symbolism of me leaving on that day. Not that I had a Jesus complex: I just liked symbolism. That, and the fact that Monica had called with good news. State's Creative Writing program had accepted me.

So I bought a plane ticket and, while I waited for Easter, practiced telling my family the news. But I never did. The day before I left I sat down and wrote two letters, one to Mama and Daddy, the other to Grandma. I told them all that I loved them, but that I was waiting for my life to begin. And it wouldn't begin till I got my butt out of Mississippi and tried to make it in the world.

"I'll miss you," I said. "I'm not sure I'm doing the right thing, and I hope you'll understand this is something I need to do. It's no reflection on you. Please don't think that. Honest."

Then I mailed the letters to Newitville, knowing they would get them the next day, but by that time I'd be on a plane.

Monica met me at the gate. She wore black jeans and a turquoise shirt with metal studs. The studs had triggered the metal detector, and as she hugged me she told me, laughing, how she had said to the security guards, "What, do you think I have a rifle under my shirt?" I tried to laugh, but I couldn't. I was thinking that Grandma, Mama and Daddy were probably fast asleep — unless they had received my letter. Then they'd be up, worried, crying, cussing, drinking (not Grandma — though she would be doing the other things.)

Monica drove me around San Francisco. It was night, and the city was having a warm spell. "It's not usually this pleasant," she said.

"Ugh," I said.

"It's rather chilly here, actually. But you'll get used to it."

"Ugh," I said. My stomach hurt, my hands were shaking. I had packed up all my clothes and moved to California. I had left Mississippi. I had actually done something HUGE that I always swore I would do.

On Market Street, Monica said. "We're near the Castro."

"Ugh."

She pointed to the balcony of a bar crowded with men. "Gays," she said, excited, like we had just spotted exotic beasts.

"Ugh."

"You don't look so well." She finally noticed. She was more excited about my arrival than I was. She was really proud of me. I did it, I actually did it. I Got Out. We both Got Out. And now, I was jobless and would be living on her couch, trying to figure out a way to pay for rent and college.

"Are you having regrets?"

I shook my head.

"Are you okay?"

I shook my head again.

"Okay, I'm going to take you home."

As soon as we got in her door, I was hit with a familiar smell — her home in Newitville. Her Pacific Heights apartment smelled of the same mixture of Chanel and eucalyptus.

"Bathroom?" I asked, holding my stomach.

She pointed down the hall. "To your left."

I ran to the bathroom, lifted the toilet seat, and threw up. I went down on my knees and felt the cool tile, so different than the worn linoleum of my grandparents bathroom and the sticky bourbon soaked floors of my parents' bathroom.

Monica stood outside the door.

"You all right?"

I had heard that when plants are moved from their environment, they go into shock. Sometimes they never recover and die. I didn't think I would die, and I hadn't thought far enough ahead to figure out how or when I would recover, but I knew that I had been removed from my environment.

What was this foreign city, this San Francisco? It seemed like the other side of the world, the moon, 10,000 leagues under the sea. I needed something familiar, something more than Monica's presence or the mixed smell of Chanel and eucalyptus. I needed a whiff of Jack Daniel's. I needed to hear my father lose his temper over an Ole Miss football game, I needed my mother to bitch about the sacrifices she made for her family. I needed to hear Grandpa mutter, "Lazy bastard," I needed to see Grandma clean the kitchen. I Got Out. I Got Out. Oh God, I actually Got Out. Now what? Success? Failure? Death? Jack Daniel's?

A voice filled my head: cousin Carson. Spring, two years ago. Grandma and Grandpa were celebrating their sixtieth wedding anniversary. Pie, Teckla and Mama threw them a party in the recreation hall of my grandparent's Presbyterian Church.

Carson drove up alone. She walked into the hall and right up to me. We had not seen each other in years.

She greeted me quoting Jean Paul Sartre. "We are condemned to be free." Her eyes were bloodshot, her voice a bit slurred, and the sweet smell of liquor drifted in the air around her, mingling politely with perfume. Even drunk, Carson could be pretentious.

"We are condemned to be free, Lisa Doodie Tingle. Remember that." Then she said, "*Tabula rasa. Carpe diem.* And all that stuff that sounds so easy and is so hard to actually do, Lisa Doodie Tingle. You know what I mean? You're a lit major. You know what I'm talking about. You're the only one here, next to me, who's gone to college — well, that is if you call Yoga college an education, but you know what I mean. You're it in your family; I'm it in mine. You understand Doodie, Lisa, Doodie Tingle?"

I wiped some spittle from my face. "I know what you mean."

But I didn't have a clue what she meant.

And as I heaved into the toilet two years later, I thought, Oh. This is what she meant. We are condemned to be free and all that stuff that sounds so easy but is so hard.

"Answer me. Are you okay?" Monica asked from the other side of the door.

"I'm fine. It's probably nerves."

"Probably."

I flushed, put the toilet lid down, and then washed my face in the sink. When I opened the door, Monica grinned big. "Well, welcome to your new home."

"Oh shit," I said and I went back into the bathroom and once again, lifted the toilet lid.

Chapter Eleven
Hoopla

The flight attendant announced, "Folks, welcome to Jackson. The local time is 8:37 pm, and it's a balmy 92 degrees."

The man in the seat behind me said, "Damn! I sure don't miss this *Mis-sippy* heat."

"Johnny, it ain't the heat, it's that God-awful humidity, sugar," the woman sitting next to him said.

"Don't I know it, doll."

When the door opened and people began filing off row by row, the couple and I stayed seated. They must have really hated the humidity. As for me, I had my reasons not to rush. I wasn't wholeheartedly looking forward to this visit. I hadn't been home since I "run away," as Grandma called my departure.

It had been a year now since I left Jackson for San Francisco. I had a job writing marketing copy in a financial firm, and at night, I took creative writing courses at San Francisco State. I now had my own studio apartment in the Tenderloin, after having lived with Monica for my first six months in San Francisco.

A year ago, after Mama got the letter I wrote telling them I was moving she called me in hysterics. In fact, Mama called me every day for the first several months after my arrival, and with each conversation, her voice grew less hysterical. "Do you have money? Are you eating? Watch out. It's a big city. They have homosexuals there."

Occasionally, my father would get on the phone. "Get your butt back on a plane and come home where you belong." He volleyed the command in a way that made it sound more like a damnation than a plea of fatherly love.

Now, I was returning home for a visit. Ava would be coming up from New Orleans with Lucy and JW and her latest husband. She had finally married Wolf/Bobby.

My parents and my grandmother met me at the gate. Grandma yelled, "Ahh, you're fat. Look at my fat baby."

I weighed 107. Some people might say that at 5'1, I was just about right for my height.

"You look fine, Doodie," Daddy said, pinching my cheek. They all three fell over me in a huge hug. Mama started to cry.

"You have lines under your eyes," she said. "I knew life out there would be too hard."

I felt my face and tried to rub away any wrinkles. I didn't realize I had them, and I suspected Mama just wanted to find me dilapidated so she could feel vindicated.

"Our little girl is getting old," Grandma said.

"She'll always be my baby." Mama cupped her hands on my cheeks. "You look tired. Are you working yourself to death?"

"No ma'am."

"Are you worried about something?"

"Worrying is your job, Mama, not mine," I said. I wondered if I could catch the next flight; I'd go anywhere. Home to San Francisco, Dallas, Atlanta, Jakarta, you name it.

"That's telling her," Daddy said. "Leave her alone, you damn hens."

We collected my bags and I sat in the back seat with Mama, who cried the entire way home because she was so happy to see me and so miserable that her baby had ran away. Grandma sat in the front and ticked off the names of people who had died in the last year. I did not know most of them, but I thought it was interesting, like she did, that Harold Armstrong died on his toilet with his pants down.

"I mean he was a proctologist," she said.

"Now that's something," Daddy said.

"It's ironic," I said.

"Oh God, my little baby." My mother cried some more. "You're all grown."

"Yeah but she grew up wrong," Daddy said.

"Pardon?" I asked.

"Well hell, look at you, living in San Francisco, damn liberal city with all them fruits. You even voted against President Reagan and he's the best president we ever had."

"Daddy, I'm a Democrat."

"Don't say that. It's just a horrible thing to say."

When we got home, Aunt Pie was sitting at the kitchen table, smoking a Camel and drinking Pabst from a can.

She took one look at me and her eyes lit up. I could tell she planned on hugging me, but first, she took a drag off her cigarette and a sip of Pabst. She held up her finger, signaling me to give her just one moment. Then she blew out the smoke and swallowed at the same time, a feat most people probably could not accomplish.

"Get over here, you little runaway." She gave me a hard hug, her bony wrist digging into my spine, then she slapped my back hard; she intended it to be a love pat, but it stung.

"Next time you want to run off to California, drag your tail over here and tell them face to face, you hear?"

Mama, standing behind me, let out a small, withered sob. Grandma said, "Now na-uh, we agreed we wouldn't make her feel bad for what she did. She knows it was wrong and doesn't need us telling her. She's home now and she's here for good."

"Grandma, I'm just here for a visit."

Grandma's brows furled. "Belle, you said she was coming home to stay."

"Lord, Mama, she's staying for a week. I told you that," Mama said.

"I'm not staying a week," I said. "I leave on Tuesday."

Now everyone's brows furled. There were so many furled brows that the room looked like a group of actors auditioning for "Days of Our Lives."

"You're just staying for a long weekend?" Mama asked.

"Yes ma'am."

"But you haven't been home for a year. You would think that after 365 days you could give us a week of your precious California time," Daddy said.

"Ava is staying a week." I said. "Mama, you confused me and Ava."

"Well I have a lot on my mind."

Daddy said, "Shit. She's bringing those damn kids down here for a week. God-damnit I won't have any peace."

Mama said, "Daddy, I think you're going to miss your war movie on HBO."

Daddy's face lit up. "I almost forgot!" He practically knocked over the table trying to get to the living room quickly. So much for him being excited about my visit. I never could compete with war movies.

Aunt Pie said, "You have broken your grandmother's heart. She's old. You know, if she has five years left, it's a miracle. You are just too big for your britches moving out to California. You're living high on the raisin. Too high if you ask me."

"Shut up Pie," Grandma said. "It's no wonder Jarvis drank himself silly." Pie's husband had died of liver cancer. Everyone in the family thought he drank himself to death because Pie drove him nuts with her constant bitching that he needed to make more money. He made more than anyone in the family. He and Pie drove a Cadillac and took hotel vacations in Florida, while my parents' idea of a trip was packing up ham sandwiches and going for a ride on the Natchez Trace.

Amazingly, Pie laughed at Grandma's jibe. It didn't bother her when people said things like this. She thought it was funny, as if it were some Henny Youngman, take-my-wife-please joke.

Mama sighed and whimpered, *again*. She said what we always said around our house when words failed. "Let's just eat."

Ava, her children and Wolf/Bobby arrived the next morning. They took over the living room, which was fine with me. I got to stay in my old room. JW and Lucy were to sleep on the couch with their feet in each other's face. I had offered to give Ava and Wolf/Bobby my old room, which had really been her old room first, but she said they'd sleep on the rollaway in the living room with the kids.

"They might get up in the middle of the night and steal something. JW is going through a phase," she told me confidentially in front of everyone as if they wouldn't hear.

"Those are bad kids," Pie said. "You should control them better."

"Uh, I'm trying," Ava said, annoyed.

So Daddy hauled the roll-away out of the walk-in closet. We had the largest closet in the county. The *Newitville Evening Post* actually wrote about it once. They said it was the size of a trailer, and I guess it was. Grandpa had built it with cedar. It was always hot inside, like a sauna, and the air stale. Small green lizards found their way in there somehow, and sometimes we would find them resting on the outside of one of the plastic dress bags where we stored our out-of-season clothes.

Evidently lizards weren't the only creatures that liked hiding in the closet. Ava's kids did as well. They burrowed themselves behind the racks of mothball soaked clothes. Wolf/Bobby kept walking to the door and saying, "Y'all okay?" to which they would yell, "This is a private club. Get out, adult!"

Everyone in the family disliked Wolf/Bobby because he didn't talk very much. My family was hard on shy people. They didn't trust them. There was something wrong with people who did not start sharing intimate details of their lives immediately. My grandmother, and my mother in particular, loved sharing their ailments with near perfect strangers. Grandma never hesitated to talk about her gout, and Mama showed no compunction about revealing the details of her recent hysterectomy, or the arthritis in her ear.

In fact, Grandma set a tone with Wolf/Bobby right off when he walked in the door. "How's your job?" she asked him. "You making money? You treat these kids right, don't you? You want children of your own? You already got these two, I know, but do you think you want your own? Two's plenty, don't you think?" A true testament to her talent, she asked her questions casually, as if she had just asked, "Do you want butter on your bread?"

Wolf/Bobby grunted his answers, which didn't help matters. Mama said, apropos of nothing, "We're having shrimp for dinner."

"I never had shrimp," he said. The boy had lived in New Orleans all of his life, and he never had shrimp. It was weird, even I thought so. But Mama took the opportunity to make a production out of this. She raised herself up from the kitchen table, and with her palms digging into the wood, said to Ava, "He's never had shrimp! He's never had shrimp!" Then she left the room, muttering, "He's never had shrimp."

Daddy yelled from the living room, where he was watching yet another war movie, "That's just not right. How could you not have had shrimp, boy?"

"I'm allergic to it," Wolf/Bobby yelled back.

"How do you know if you are allergic to shrimp if you have never had it?"

"My mama told me."

"I forget, are you Catholic?" Grandma asked. This meant something. Just what I'm not sure.

"*Nosum*," he said, which was his way of saying "No sir ma'am."

"Ah-haw," Grandma said as if his response explained something.

I slipped into the living room, pretending to look interested in the fight JW and Lucy were having behind Daddy's easy chair. He had just called her a whore. She retaliated, calling him a dick head. Ava yelled from the kitchen, her mother-radar fine-tuned. "Shut up will you." She may have been talking to our family, though.

Mama showed up at the dinner table drunk. She slurred her incomprehensible words and sat in her chair, smiling at nothing. Grandma made her move to the children's table, which we had set up on the other side of the kitchen. Only a half-counter divided what we called the "dining room" and the kitchen, so we could all hear and see one another, which was good, because shortly after Mama joined me, JW and Lucy, she passed out face down in the shrimp Creole. Grandma started screaming. Lucy and JW laughed. Daddy cursed. He and Wolf/Bobby carried her to bed, rice stuck to her cheek. They pulled back the covers and found an empty fifth of Jack Daniel's.

"Holy shit, I just bought that yesterday," Daddy said.

After a little hysteria from Grandma and Ava, and much discussion, we decided to take her to the hospital.

The doctor said she had alcohol poisoning and Daddy said, "Hell, not again."

"What do you mean, not again?" I said.

"Nothing." And he waved his hand at me, signifying that was all the information I would get.

Mama spent the night at the hospital. Everyone fussed about who would stay with her. Grandma wanted to because she was her mother. Daddy didn't want to; you could tell he didn't like the idea, but he didn't want to seem uncaring, as Grandma would ride him on that till the end of eternity. Actually, we all would.

"Oh, hell. She's my wife. I'll stay," he said. To which we all said, "Nooo, nooo. That's okay." He'd be too unbearably grouchy the next day for any of us to bear. We'd rather lose sleep.

Ava was the only one who stated outright that she wouldn't stay.

"I can't leave those kids of mine alone. They'll burn down the house or something."

"I'll stay," I said, and no one objected. Maybe it's because I sounded sincere. I wanted to stay, but my motives weren't pure. I thought I could get more sleep. Mama was out of it the entire time, coming to only every now and then to say things like, "That boy never had shrimp," and "Put on some Sinatra, will you sugar? I want to sing along."

Mainly she snored and it took me a while to get comfortable. So I watched an old movie on the TV hanging high on the wall. *Hush Hush Sweet Charlotte*. When an incredulous Betty Davis asked a guileful Olivia de Havilland, "Hell, do you think I invited you down here for your company?" I got misty-eyed, even though the moment wasn't meant to provoke tears. I just knew how it felt to be stuck in a house with someone who frequently misunderstood your intentions.

Mama woke up around six o'clock the next morning. She leaned over and jabbed me on my shin with her foot. My legs were stretched between the chair where I had slept and the aluminum rail of her bed. She could barely talk above a whisper, "Why did you send us a letter instead of telling us in person that you were moving out to California?"

"Mama . . . I told you the first time I called from San Francisco. I just didn't have the nerve. I knew you would cry and get all hysterical."

"When have I ever gotten hysterical?" She raised herself up a little, miffed.

"When haven't you?"

"I'm never hysterical. I just get upset because I have so much on my mind."

"You've always had a lot on your mind."

"I know. My whole life. Things haven't been easy for me, having to work so hard and me and your father living under the same roof with Mama and Daddy like we did all those years, listening to their constant criticisms of our drinking. It's the craziness of this family. It's worn me out and maybe that's made me seem like I drank too much, but honest, I never drank that much. I was just tired after all the hoopla."

"You did drink a lot."

"Well I had a lot on my mind."

"Okay, Mama, that's fine. Please rest. You're in the hospital."

"I know. I had a minor stroke. It's all the stress this family gives me."

"You did not have a stroke. You are suffering from alcohol poisoning."

"I only had two drinks."

"Yes ma'am. The first half of the bottle and the second half."

"Don't be disrespectful. My head hurts and it feels like I have clay running through my veins. Anyway, you don't know what my life is like."

"Yes ma'am."

"Grandma says you left Mississippi because of me."

"I left because I wanted more out of life than I could get down here."

Mama blew out a sigh. "You really are too big for your britches. You did not get that from me. You got that from your grandfather. God rest that old bastard's soul."

"Yes ma'am."

Later that morning, I left the hospital in the Belle-Mobile and performed a ritual I performed many times when I lived in Mississippi. I drove across the Mississippi River Bridge, the radio turned up loud, the windows rolled down so the cold air could rush in, and I pretended I was going to keep going until I hit California. When I got about five miles across the bridge, I turned around and drove toward home. When I got there, I kept going, then I turned onto Old Highway 80 and drove east toward Jackson, like I was going to the airport, like I was going to get on a plane and fly away. At Bovina, I turned around and came home.

Lucy was playing with a hula-hoop in the back yard as I pulled up and parked. We didn't have a garage, just a wide gravel space behind the house where we kept the cars.

"Can you keep a secret?" she asked me. She was shaking her hips inside the hula-hoop. It had been mine when I was a kid; she had found it somewhere. I couldn't help but feel possessive for a moment, like she was stealing a piece of my childhood.

"I can keep a secret."

"I'm pregnant."

"You aren't pregnant. You're nine."

"I had sex with a boy," she said. "Don't tell anyone. I feel I can trust you because Mama said you are a big whore."

"Your mother called me a whore?"

"No, she just said you would never settle down, and I know that's code for whore."

"No it's not."

"Whatever. Don't tell her about me being pregnant, though, okay? What do I do?"

"You're late then?"

"Late for what?"

"Your period."

"No. Well, I don't know. Most girls don't get their period for another couple of years. You ought to know that. You're so old and all."

I saw that we had a miscommunication problem, a family trait. "So you haven't even ever gotten your period."

"Right."

"Then you aren't pregnant."

"So I can screw boys till I get my period?"

"No. Don't have sex. You are way too young. You should be playing with Barbies."

"Can I tell you something?"

"Yes."

"Got you! I'm not having sex! Haha." She tossed the hula-hoop aside and danced around me a little. "I got you good."

"That's funny." I wanted to go home to San Francisco. Even the children were fraying my nerves. Monica said she could never go back to Newitville because it made her feel trapped. I thought she was being overly dramatic, but now I understood.

Inside the house, Daddy and Grandma sat around the table. Grandma informed me that Wolf/Bobby had driven to Jackson to "waste money on nonsense." I didn't ask. Ava washed dishes silently at the sink, staring into the water in a way that reminded me of Mama. JW stood by the microwave looking inside the glass. Lightening bolts darted around inside.

"Cool," he said.

Daddy leaped up and yanked the microwave door open and pulled out a metal pan filled with Shrimp Creole leftovers. "Na-ah, you damn moron. What's wrong with you? You aren't right in the head."

JW laughed and pointed at Daddy, who had turned purple with anger. He said, "Your eyes are bulging now."

"YOU ARE AN IDIOT CHILD. YOU DON'T PUT METAL IN A MICROWAVE!"

My father's yelling immediately triggered a memory I had pushed away from long ago. We were in the kitchen, me, Daddy, Mama, Grandma. Grandpa was still alive and he was napping in bed. Daddy sat at the kitchen table, reading the paper. Mama and Grandma were canning tomatoes at the counter. I was sitting across from my father at the table, working on college and financial aid applications. Daddy thought I was applying to Ole Miss, but I had other plans. I was writing an essay to get into Berkeley.

I didn't care if they caught me filling out the applications. If they asked why, I'd tell them it was their fault, with all their drinking, and their fighting with my grandparents and basically making our home as hospitable as a parking lot.

Lately, I had been feeling particularly rebellious, letting my boyfriend get a little more intimate than I really wanted, and drinking one more Miller Pony's than I really thought best on our nights out. I had every intention of being a bad kid and getting in some sort of minor trouble just to up my parent's agony; then, just when the heat got to be too high, I'd fly off to college and begin a dewy, new, untarnished life.

Of course, I didn't think out my plan very well. I omitted details of my future, such as where I'd get the money for the plane ticket. As for college itself, I was counting heavily on government aid, because I knew my parents couldn't afford it.

"Doodie, get me a glass of tea," Daddy had asked me. I put my pencil down and gave him a look, trying to let him know I thought he was lazy for not getting the drink himself. I filled a glass with ice and as I poured tea inside I lost my grip and the glass fell to the floor and shattered. Ice, tea, and broken glass were everywhere.

"God-damn it, be more careful," Daddy yelled.

"Fuck you!" I said, just blurting it out.

"Pick up the Goddamn mess," Daddy said. "And give me some more tea."

He shook his finger at me, his face turning purple. He bunched the paper up and threw it across the table. "Shib," he said, which I think was a cross between shit and bitch.

The memory left as Daddy continued his tirade against JW.

"Jesus Christ you aren't right in the head! ARE YOU? ANSWER ME!" Daddy was now screaming. He stood over JW and the boy looked up at him, his lower lip trembling.

"Answer your grandfather, JW," Ava said, her voice calm and bored.

"I'm right in the head, you old bastard," JW said.

Daddy reached to out to slap him across the face, but I grabbed his hand. Our eyes met. I squeezed his wrist hard, with strength I didn't realize I had. I thought of that episode with the dropped tea glass and understood the inadequacy of my "Fuck you," response. I could say more to him with the look in my eyes. I could say it all, in fact. *If you didn't want me to leave Mississippi, then why didn't you change? Why didn't you help Mama change? You hated living in this house with Grandma and Grandpa. Why were you too weak to move?* And I also said, *You may have been too weak, old man, but I am not, nor will I ever be. Because I watched you and I'm doing the opposite with my life.*

Grandma swept up next to us. "No one hits any of the children in this family as long as I'm around," she said.

Then she hauled back and punched Daddy in the stomach. He grabbed his belly and a string of invectives flew off his tongue and the next thing I knew, he was out the back door, getting into his truck and peeling down the driveway.

Something weird happened to me. My muscles shook, like a band loosening, and I started to cry. I was embarrassed to cry, too, which edged me toward a wail. It may be hard to believe, but my family had not seen me really, truly cry since I was a child. Mama cried so much, over little things like broken glasses and private things that she wouldn't reveal. Grandma rarely cried. "Crying is useless," she'd say. "If you've got the blues, work them away." Grandma must have had some major-league blues: she had the largest garden on our road, and she worked it with the zeal of a religious fanatic.

I think the last time I had cried in front of them was in the third grade, when I found a king snake coiled up in a vanity drawer in my playhouse in the back yard. Grandpa and Daddy had built this extravagant structure as a birthday gift to me, an enormous act of love considering they did it without every saying a word to each other. Grandma and Mama ran interference and even orchestrated the concept.

I had come running into the house crying, freaked from the snake. Grandma grabbed her hoe, Grandpa grabbed his shotgun. The snake was killed, the vanity destroyed. It looked like a murder had been committed in there. Afterwards, when I played with my dolls in my playhouse, I held up Ken in one hand who said to Barbie in my other hand, "I love your wallpaper design," which was really blood spots from the slain snake.

Grandma tried to soothe me after Daddy left. "That old bastard made you cry, darling."

"It not just Daddy, it's Mama and, hell, it's you and it's these bratty kids and it's her." I pointed at Ava.

Everyone started protesting. Grandma called me an ingrate, after all the things she had done for me over the years. Lucy said, "I'm just a kid, I'm not a brat you old bag." JW said, "Aunt Lisa is mean" and Ava said, "You bother me, too, Lisa." I put my hands over my face and yowled, "I NEVER WANT TO SEE ANY OF YOU AGAIN."

Some noise came out of my mouth from deep in my bowels, some sort of audible emotion, a constipation of the soul maybe let loose by a purge of rage.

Ava grabbed my hand and took me into my parents' bathroom. She put the toilet lid down and sat down, then sat me on her knee.

"I don't hold none of this against you, Lisa. You have your little breakdown. It's your turn. These people are crazy and they've made me loony, too. Look at me and learn, because I'm you in another ten years. I stopped eating for five years because of these damn nuts. I've been married so much I can't count the times, and I'm not even thirty-five. I wake up in the middle of the night shaking because I have nightmares. And it's all their fault. Everything bad is their fault."

"No, it's not all their fault. We should get over this stuff. It's up to us to move on."

"We don't have the genes to move on."

"But it wasn't all bad."

"The good wasn't that good."

She was wrong. There were very good times. Like the day Grandpa and Daddy finished building my playhouse. Grandma poured ginger ale in a punch bowl and dropped spoonfuls of orange sherbet inside. She placed it on an old TV tray in the center of the playhouse. We all sat on the floor and drank punch from little glass cups. Daddy and Grandpa didn't talk to each other, but that was okay. Their silence defined them, like my mother being an alcoholic defined her. It's the way things were, so it didn't matter.

But I guess it did; it all mattered in small increments that led to this moment, where I sat on my sister's knee on the toilet in our parents' bathroom and bathroom, crying.

Grandma walked in. "I'm not mad at you," she said. "Your old mama is in the hospital for being a drunk and let's face it, it's hard being tough around all this weakness. You take after me, thank God. You know what I hate most about you moving out to San Francisco?"

I shook my head.

"There's more people out there and more people means you are exposed to more nuts. People are not inherently good, don't ever let any idiot tell you otherwise. People are inherently weak. They are just trying to do what's best for them, and what's best for them at any given time can hurt you. There will be people who try to break you because breaking you is the only way they can feel good. Don't let them feel good, Lisa. Let them be miserable and you just move on."

And with that, she walked out the door. I sat on Ava's lap, letting the final tears trickle away. Neither of us said a word. It was as if Grandma had just come in and administered a shot meant to heal, but we couldn't figure out exactly what the medicine would cure.

After a few minutes, Ava said, "Let's go get an ice cream cone."

"Do your kids have to come?" I asked, wiping a hand across my cheek. "No offense. They just make me nervous."

"None taken. They make me nervous too."

We ate donuts and ice cream at Shipley's Donuts, then we went to Sonic Drive-in and ate onion rings and French fries. When we came home, Daddy had picked up Mama from the hospital. Grandma cooked dinner, baked chicken and fresh tomato and cucumber salad with store-bought rolls she warmed in the oven. We ate quietly, even the kids were quiet. Then Ava and I cleaned up the dishes, Grandma took her bath, and Mama and Daddy and the rest of them went into the living room and watched television.

After a while, me and Ava and Grandma joined them. We watched television till people started going to bed, one by one, first Grandma, then Mama, then Daddy and finally me, saying "Sleep tight," to Ava and her clan. JW responded, "Don't let the bed bugs bite."

But before that, while we watched television, none of us had mentioned what happened that afternoon, or Mama's drinking. We all sat in the crowded living room, the chairs pushed around the massive rollaway bed, and watched a movie. I don't remember which movie, but I know that no one laughed, no one cried, no one said a word. We just stared at the screen. It was the nicest family moment I could recall having had in years.

Chapter Twelve
Sinatra Generation

In 1991, Sinatra played the Desert Inn in Las Vegas, and as a treat to my parents, I offered them an all-expenses paid trip to see him. It was also a way for me to spend some quality time with them, since I only saw Mama and Daddy about once or twice a year, and each visit lasted only a few days.

Going to see Sinatra seemed fitting. He had always been part of our lives, at least his music had, and my parents' admiration hadn't waned since the forties. But there was one true, huge underlying reason I offered the trip: I feared they wouldn't be around much longer, my parents or Sinatra.

The large age gap between me and my parents showed the consequence of differences. Barely in my thirties, I had senior citizen parents experiencing health issues associated with people closer to ninety than sixty.

A year earlier, my father had been diagnosed with colon cancer and treated. His doctor had since declared him free and clear, though he'd wear a colostomy bag the rest of his life.

My mother had been ill, too, suffering from small strokes, which had thankfully finally forced her to stop drinking. But the effect of the strokes had an ironic effect on Mama. She seemed drunk all the time. She slurred her words, had an unsteady balance, and her eyes had the look of someone waiting for one last highball after a long night of cocktails.

Grandma had recently died peacefully in her sleep. She was 95. Mama reacted to her death as she had to Grandpa's. She seemed lost without her parents there to judge her. It was almost like now that they were gone, she had no one to disappoint, and hence, no purpose in life.

As for Sinatra, he was getting on in years and though his health was reportedly okay, decades of drinking and smoking surely had taken its toll. I figured he'd outlast my parents, but I also knew this could be his last tour.

I truly believed Mama would go before Daddy. She was the more feeble, though Daddy now sounded like an old man, hoary, each word a mouthful of gravel.

The investment firm where I worked had a good year. I now headed up the communication's department, and I received a larger-than-expected bonus that Christmas. I was feeling rich and in love because about six months before Grandma passed, I married a handsome young French gentleman, a chef in San Francisco. His name was Philip Dubois, just like Blanche from Streetcar Named Desire. Philip looked like Bruce Springsteen if Bruce wore expensive clothes. Philip cared about all the details, from the quality of his shoes to living every moment of his life full throttle. So we drank good wine, ate great food and Philip pitched me woo as if he were the zealot who created woo.

Monica didn't think we would last because I had transferred my high-school crush onto my husband.

"I've heard of women marrying men who remind them of their father, but never this," she had said.

But she was wrong because I loved him and he loved me and as far as Philip and I were concerned, we were the greatest couple that ever existed.

After I got that large Christmas bonus, Philip suggested that I take an extra thousand of the money and buy my parents a trip to Vegas — just the three of us. We still had that generosity young couples have with each other.

"You'll be happy you had this time, one day," he said. "One day" was my parents' code now for "after death" and Philip and I had invariably incorporated it into our vocabulary. Daddy would say something like, "I want you to have my collection of Civil War Times . . . one day." Or Mama would say, "This damn rundown house will be yours and your sister's, one day." In pensive moments, which were increasing in occurrence and velocity, she would tell me, "You'll be all alone one day, just you and your sister."

Everything fell into place: the bonus, Philip's suggestion that I take my parent's to Vegas, the fact that Sinatra was playing the Desert Inn.

It was the best gift I could give my parents. Mama and Daddy's fervent love for the man got weird at times — even more so than my teenage passion for Bruce Springsteen. My parents never had money to send me or Ava to college — I needed scholarships, loans and government grants — but they always had money for Sinatra. They had flown around the country to see him over the years, adding to their mounting debt that had now grown to ten thousand. Once I had told Daddy that I wanted braces for my lower teeth. He laughed and said they couldn't afford them. This was right after they had flown to Vegas to see Sinatra in Vegas.

"You can afford to go fly off to see Sinatra," I said.

"Yeah, but that's different," he said.

"How?"

He looked at me like I was stupid. "It's Sinatra," he said, and shrugged me off. "We work hard, and this is how we reward ourselves."

Fortunately, I didn't really need braces and, to Daddy's credit, he knew that. I was just going through a phase where all my buddies had braces so I wanted them. But sometimes, though, I wondered the big "What if?" If I had really needed those braces, or some sort of medical attention, would my parents have spent the money instead on Frank Sinatra?

At first Daddy didn't want to go. In fact, he dropped a bomb.

"Oh Doodie," he said, "Your mother and I owe $10,000 to creditors. If anything, I'd have you put the money toward that."

"You want me to spend my hard earned money to get you out of debt?"

"Well, we could use some help."

"How did you get so far in debt?" then I quickly added, "Never mind. I know."

It wasn't just the trips to see Sinatra. They rewarded themselves, whether they could afford that reward or not, with new cars, like the Belle-Mobile, their large brown land yacht. Instead of shopping at Sears or JC Penney, they shopped at Floyds, a privately owned, highly marked-up department store. And then there were the bottles and bottles of Jack Daniel's they stockpiled, or the dinners at nice restaurants punctuated more with highballs than food.

"I don't see why you are so angry," Daddy said.

"I've worked hard for that bonus money, and gee, somehow the idea of paying off your liquor bill angers me. All my other friends get God-damn handouts from their parents, whether it's help in a financial crunch or a down payment on a house. But you live off social security checks and your VA pension."

The part I left out was how several times over the years, Daddy had phoned me and asked for help on a particular bill. I had to overnight money once so they wouldn't have their lights cut off. Another time, it was the phone. I had to pay down their debt to the drugstore so Mama could get her medicine.

If they spent all their money on little luxuries, the luxury that made them the happiest had been Sinatra's concerts. They returned from each event enlivened like teenagers. Their words had more punch; their energy . . . well, they had energy, lots of it. Sinatra reminded them of their youth.

Things got done after a trip to see their hero perform. The house got painted, the roof fixed, their drinking even slowed down. They didn't need the lift that alcohol gave them.

Daddy and I let an uncomfortable silence ring between us for too long a moment. We were playing chicken with who would speak first, both of us wanting to apologize.

"Okay, I'll send you money," I said. "I'll send you what the trip would have cost."

"Oh hell, what am I thinking?" Daddy said. "We won't be around forever, and if the bills aren't paid, they aren't paid. The bill collectors can't come after us once we're gone. We'd love to go to Vegas, Doodie. Thank you. Thank you so much." And there it was, that young voice, the old man disappearing at the mere notion of seeing Sinatra perform.

I should have hated Sinatra, if for no other reason than as an act of rebellion against my parents. But while my friends discovered punk in the late seventies and New Wave in the eighties, and then grunge in the nineties, I listened to *In the Wee Small Hours, Only the Lonely, Song For Swinging Lovers, Come Fly with Me.* Then there was my favorite, the one that made me understand that my inheritance, a love for Sinatra, was worth more than money: *Sinatra and Basie.*

And my parents' favorite record? *Sinatra at the Sands.*

But if I loved his music, Mama and Daddy were in love with the image he portrayed. They giggled like girls with crushes over his cool ring-a-ding swagger. Of course, during the sixties, the Rat Pack made drinking part of their Las Vegas stage act, rolling a liquor cart onto the Sands stage and making glib remarks about "mixing a salad" or "making a sandwich," both euphemisms for concocting cocktails.

Later, in biographies, I'd read that they weren't really drinking, that those bottles were filled with iced tea. Maybe. I'd seen pictures of Sinatra on stage drinking a beer, with a one-inch head of foam at the top. It didn't look like iced tea to me. When my parents saw him drink, whether it was photographs or on television, they would smile at each other, like they were in on the joke. Sinatra made drinking cool; he validated my parents' favorite pastime.

But still, when I heard Sinatra really didn't drink as much as purported, I got mad. It felt like a betrayal to my parents, as if he personally had set them up and said, "Look at how much fun I'm having. Gee, I think I'll have another cocktail." And my parents, more like children than adults in their adulation, followed suit wholeheartedly. I viewed my parents' life as a waste, a futile attempt at glamour.

Yet I loved Sinatra. Ultimately, I guess I loved him because his music proved to be one of the few things I had in common with my parents. If nothing else, we had Frank.

My parents arrived in Vegas before I did. By the time I got to the hotel, they were in a bad mood. Daddy was hungry, and Mama had insisted that they wait for me. A good appetite was a thing of the past for them, so when Daddy did have the desire to eat, it was urgent. We hunkered down in a booth at the buffet café in Desert Inn.

I noticed flies flitting over the salad bar and opted to go for hot cooked vegetables instead. My father loaded his plate with ribs, mashed potatoes and, cornbread stuffing, and pasta salad: the latter he claimed made his meal healthy. I didn't even question his logic. It was a Rodneyism, as Mama and I called his quirks of reason.

Mama plopped a skimpy tablespoon of beans and carrots on her plate and then sat at the table looking around, dazed from her drugs and generally seeming satisfied.

"It's good to see you," she said, looking at me. It was the third time she said it in an hour.

"You too."

"I sure miss my little Doodie. We keep hoping you'll move home."

"Well, California is my home," I said. We had had this conversation many times before. I was married for God's sake, with a condo and a job. Yet my parents kept inquiring as to when I would return "home," like Alzheimer's patients who, right after they've just had dinner, ask, "When can we eat?"

"Hell, California ain't your home," Daddy said and took an angry bite of ribs.

The conversation did not improve. I tried to think of things to say, but I found that whenever I talked about my life in California, it worried them. They didn't like to hear about all the restaurants or plays I could go to, because they were concerned I would get mugged, or as Mama put it, "attacked."

Work was off limits. They did not understand what a corporate writer did.

"You type," Daddy would say, the few times I tried to explain it. "So you're a secretary."

"I'm not a secretary."

"Do you answer phones?"

"I write things like marketing brochures and proposals and speeches."

"Ah-huh," Daddy said, and they looked at each other like they had just raised a liar.

So we did what we always did when we couldn't find any common ground. We talked about Frank Sinatra.

Kitty Kelly had written an expose on him and I had burned through every page, half-believing it and loving every word, true or false. I told them of the gossip, the actresses Sinatra bedded, the Rat Pack antics, the rumor that he'd slept with Nancy Reagan when she was first lady.

"Now I just don't believe that," Mama said.

"Hell, neither do I," Daddy said, "Nancy Reagan is not a good-looking woman. Sinatra can do better. Even at his age."

When we finished our meal, we returned to their room and watched reruns of shows that we'd seen before; their favorites, like "Crazy Like a Fox" or "Highway to Heaven." We didn't talk. In fact, we took turns inadvertently napping in front of the TV.

At first, I could not remember the last time I felt this bored, then I remembered, it was the last time I visited them. Watching television is what we did. Hours of it. It seems every show was always a rerun, too, as if new programming didn't exist. I think I've only seen one episode of "Murder She Wrote," but I've seen it countless times, and always with Mama and Daddy. It's the one with actors in a community theater. The bitchy lead gets murdered.

I looked at my parents as they snoozed while that same episode of "Murder She Wrote" blasted from the tube once again. I wondered how it came to be that I was the daughter of this snoring woman and this tossing and turning man. I couldn't recall ever feeling close to them, but I know there was a time when we had more to say to each other. But even then, the relationship wasn't honest. As a teen, I'd make small talk to butter them up so I could get the car on Saturday night or get money for new clothes. The only thing I really knew about them now was that they were sick, tired of being poor, consumed with the thought of death or going into a nursing home or getting more ill, and that they loved Sinatra and the Ole Miss Rebels football team. Those few things summed up their existence.

It thrilled my father that we had to bribe the maitre d' for a good table at the show. "Just like every Sinatra show ever," he said, beaming. "Some things never change."

We had paid a man name Joseph twenty dollars to get closer to the stage. He wore a red waistcoat with red buttons and looked about seventy. Joseph never looked at us, he simply took our money without a word and put us at the end of a table for ten — the end farthest from the stage. We were on the first row of the second level, only twenty feet from the stage. We found out the couple at the other end of the table only paid him ten dollars and got better seats.

"Damn mobster," Daddy said. I could tell he was actually pleased by Joseph's slight, the whole illicit angle gave him a kick.

When Sinatra came out, the room buzzed with grown adults in awe of a legend. I sat there watching, wanting to remember every moment, because I was witnessing history. I could picture myself at ninety saying to a circle of youngsters at my feet, "Yes, I saw Sinatra. I was so close to him I could almost touch him." What I would forget is the way he looked — his old blue eyes without their zing, a little scared, almost like he had just woken up, found himself on stage, and instinctively knew he belonged there but wasn't sure what exactly was happening.

His set started with "I've Got the World on a String" and at first, the evening looked promising. His voice, full, strong, a baritone of riches, was there; the classic ring-a-ding Sinatra. He followed it with "I've Got You Under My Skin," and the voice broke, flat. The Chairman only had one good song in him.

I don't think most of the room noticed or cared. Sinatra had been in their lives for probably fifty or sixty years, he was family and could be forgiven for an overly cured voice. There were more Word War II veterans in there than at a VFW meeting.

At one point, Mama leaned over, smiled at me, and squeezed my hand. Her eyes were full of her tears. She loved to cry. Tonight, I understood. I could have teared up myself. This man who had been in the background of our world for all my life and most of theirs was in the flesh with us tonight, and he was so blatantly imperfect and old. Like he should be, like any surrogate relative of ours would be just by virtue of being a Tingle family relative, albeit a surrogate one.

After a few songs, Sinatra held up a large glass of amber liquid and said, "*Cintani*. 100 years." And he took a long sip, telling us it was Jack Daniel's, straight up. It looked like iced tea to me; a little too brown. My parents had never been without a bottle of Jack Daniel's in my youth, I knew the exact color. It, too, was like a relative to us, its presence so constant.

Maybe it really was Jack Daniel's because the more he sang, the more he relied on the teleprompter. At one point near the end of the evening, he forgot the words to "My Way." The audience, adoring, faithful, took over and the entire room sang the words for him, using the punctuated phrasing he once used, as best as they could.

Sinatra's old blue eyes clouded and watered. He had to sit back on his stool, overwhelmed. My parents exchanged glances, smiling, both obviously touched that he was touched by his fans. It was a Hallmark moment, a tearjerker commercial, and all of us loved it. We sang louder, off key, ear-piercing, dog-yowling. It was beautiful. We were, as was our hero, delighting in our faultiness. We were all frayed electrical wires, buzzing, zapping, blue sparks of disarray, and everyone in love with everyone else.

Later, the reality of what had happened hit my father. We walked slowly out of the room. I held onto Daddy's elbow. He looked dazed.

"He's so old," Daddy muttered. "Just so old." He shook his head, sadly.

Daddy probably knew this would be the last time he'd ever see him. He and Mama were getting too old for trips like this. I think there was something else: I don't believe Daddy expected Sinatra to grow old. It was almost as if as long as he stayed young, so would Daddy. He said to me, "I'm going to die sooner than later." He had said things like this many times before. This time he understood it.

We found a café off from the main casino and sat there, slowly eating coconut crème pie. I tried to get a conversation going by asking Daddy what was his favorite time of life. I expected him to say the fifties, when he was going to clubs and hearing all the greats in their prime:

He said, "The seventies."

I had not expected that. I asked him why.

"I had both of you kids and I was still young enough to enjoy you." He paused. "You know, children really do make your life. It's a precious time."

"Precious" was not a word he used often, if ever. He must have meant it.

After dessert, my parents went to bed, I decided to walk the casino floor and people watch. I got a weak vodka and grapefruit and played a game with myself: count the fat people with bad hair. I had counted over fifty, when I turned a corner and saw a small crowd huddled around a craps table. There was a familiar buzz around these people, and as I got nearer, I saw Sinatra in the middle, rolling the dice. He looked tired but determined to stay awake. A real glass of Jack Daniel's sat in front of him. I just knew the real thing when I saw it.

I hung back and waited. Eventually he got up to leave, and I approached him. I explained that my parents had been huge fans since the forties. He didn't seem surprised and I'm sure he had heard many similar stories before. I handed him the cocktail napkin that had been wrapped around my vodka, and I got a pen out of my purse. "Please, would you give them your autograph."

"Sure, kid," he said. I blushed — he spoke to me! He wrote, "From one old geezer to two others, thanks for listening, FS." Then he moved on, as if the conversation hadn't even taken place.

First thing the next morning, I showed the napkin to Mama and Daddy. They did not believe that this was really Frank Sinatra's autograph. They giggled like teens and for a few minutes looked young again. It took some convincing, but they finally believed me. I put a lot of stock in the power of that autograph just then. I had fantasies that the rest of the trip would be happy, we'd talk and laugh, there would be no discussion of old age, disease, or death. The autograph was a turning point. Frank Sinatra had the power to make my family if not young, then youthful.

"I'll be damned," Daddy said, finally understanding that I had met his hero.

"This is probably worth something, "Mama said, sniffing it like she was hunting for Sinatra's scent.

Daddy took the napkin from my hands and stared at it like it was treasure. Gently raising it up in a hand that shook slightly, he said, "This will be yours one day, you hear?"

Chapter Thirteen
Myths of the Modern South

Many years ago in Newitville, a couple of teenagers were out on a date one night. They were necking in the deserted parking lot of Mint Springs, where confederates once fought Northern troops during our town's siege. The girl heard something outside her boyfriend's car and asked him to check on it.

He got out and a minute later she heard a loud thump. She called his name; there was no answer. She called him again and again, but he didn't respond. She knew something was wrong and, just as she was about to lock the car, his bloody body plunked down on the windshield with a loud thud. He bounced off and rolled onto the ground.

Screaming, she slid over to the driver's seat and backed out of the parking lot before doing a U-turn onto the street, screeching away. When she reached home, she got out of the car and fainted right there in the driveway: she'd seen a silver hand hook attached to the outside car door handle.

Thus started the legend of the Newitville hook-man, who preyed on teenage couples making out in dark, desolate locations.

My father used to tell me this story when I was growing up, which upset my grandmother. She believed I shouldn't hear such things because Satan would invade my dreams and cause nightmares. Daddy maintained that the story had a moral, and that when I started dating, I'd know better than to neck with boys.

Of course, when I got old enough for such things, the story didn't stop me. It just stopped me from necking with boys at night in the parking lot of Mint Springs.

For my father's 81st birthday Philip and I flew down from San Francisco. My parents had had a bad year. Mama had another stroke that January, her second one in six months. Both had been minor, but she wasn't thinking clearly. Daddy had not felt well for many months. He had stomach pains and often felt feverish. He had undergone tests, but nothing showed up.

The day after our arrival, a Monday, he underwent more tests at Newitville Medical Center. Philip and I had planned to stay in Newitville till the results came in, then we would drive down to New Orleans for a vacation.

The doctor discovered a large tumor growing inside my father's belly. It stretched up into his esophagus. A similar test months earlier had shown nothing.

"It's a wildfire tumor," Dr. Kelly told my mother and me. She misheard him and thought he said, "wildflower." She later told me that she had thought it was a lovely name to give death. Aunt Teckla was with us when we got the news.

"You can fix it, right?" she asked the doctor, as if Daddy's tumor was nothing more than a worn car fan belt.

"This tumor is inoperable," Dr. Kelly said, "there's nothing we can do. He doesn't have long. Maybe two months, maybe four."

Teckla grabbed my hand. The news floated over me.

"That rascal is always getting into some sort of trouble," Mama said. Then she got teary-eyed. "I told him to take better care of himself. He's just so stubborn, though. Damn him!"

The attendant wheeled Daddy into a private room, where he would stay for a few days for more tests. He had tears in his eyes. "My throat hurts," he said. Maybe his throat really did hurt; they had stuck a small tube with a monitor down it to see the tumor. I think he had the tears, though, because he knew that the birthday we celebrated the day before, would be his last.

Philip and I debated whether we should stay in Newitville and forget New Orleans. Mama and Daddy encouraged us to go and enjoy our vacation.

"You can come back in a few weeks, maybe," Daddy said. "I'll need some help with things, you know." "You know" meant handling his affairs, specifically, closing down his life.

On the way out of town, we stopped at George Latourno's office, my parent's attorney. George had been a family friend since I was child. My parents never really had any need to use him, but they called him their attorney anyway. Truthfully, he wasn't that good a friend, but a fellow member of their church. I asked him what I needed to do in order to settle my father's affairs.

"You need to move home," he said.

"California is my home."

He slit his eyes and sucked air through his teeth, like I had just caused him physical pain. "California is not your home. You are a Mississippian, don't you forget that, young lady. California is not a place you call home. Newitville is, and your parents need you."

I tried to explain that, in fact, my life was entrenched out West. We owned a home, Philip had his career and I had mine. We could not just drop things and move to Newitville, where the major industry was casino gambling and Civil War tourism. It was a place where the ghost of General Grant haunted the crap tables at Harrah's.

"There's nothing for us here," I said.

"Your family is here," George said.

Despite his vitriol, he gave me a list of things I needed to do. I had to get Daddy's social security and VA benefits information. My mother was entitled to some of these benefits after he died, so I needed the right forms. I also needed to close out any credit cards and try to pay them off. Daddy still had the same $10,000 debt. George said I might consider selling their property.

"You'll want your mother to live with you, of course, after your father goes." His eyes fired a warning shot should I consider disagreeing.

It wasn't until we got back in our rented white Corolla and were well on our way to New Orleans that the impact of everything hit me. My father was dying; I had to close down his life.

Once, a girl water-skiing in Century Lake right across the river in the Louisiana Delta, plowed right into a nest of water moccasins. Witnesses said it looked like the muddy water was boiling as the snakes attacked her. The girl managed to free herself and her friends pulled her from the water. She was dead by the time they laid her on the deck, her body covered in welts that looked like wasp stings.

The story changed over the years. Sometimes it wasn't a girl who fell in the snakes' nest, but a guy, or an old man, or a mother of three. The location changed, too, depending on what part of the South you heard the story. Sometimes it was a murky lake outside of New Orleans, or the silt-heavy Mississippi River up near Memphis, or a bottomless reservoir in Alabama, or even the Yazoo River, which slithered through the Delta.

Philip and I stood under cover from the hissing rain inside the concrete pavilion in New Orleans' Audubon Park. Around us, tall ancient oaks glistened. The story of the snakes floated in fragments in my head. Daddy told it to me, another morality tale, one against the dangers of water-skiing, a popular Newitville sport. And, of course, as a warning about snakes.

At the same time as I was half-thinking about his tale, I called Dr. Kelly on a pay phone to ask if I should come back now or later or when.

"There's not much you can do. Your daddy needs to stay in the hospital for a while. Your mother, I'm afraid, needs to go into a nursing home. She's just not well, you know that."

I was silent, unsure of what to say. This latest news overwhelmed me even more. My head felt soggy from ear to ear. We had left the hospital fairly quickly that morning. It was my fault, I guess, even though I had volunteered to stay. I couldn't deal with the emotion of all this illness. I knew my parents were alone and terrified. They didn't have much money and, frankly, we had been planning my mother's death more than my father's.

"Can we wait till after Daddy dies before we put Mama in a home?"

"If your father has to worry about your mother, it'll kill him sooner. I'll get you the names and numbers of the appropriate people to call at the nursing homes around here.

I know there are waiting lists, so I'll do what I can to help speed up the process."

I was grateful for his kindness, even if it meant committing an act of supreme unkindness toward my mother. I had a faint image of my mother rocking in a chair in a room made of lime green cinder blocks, her eyes glazed from too many sedatives.

For a few years now, my parents had mentioned nursing homes in the course of discussing their fate. They pronounced the word the way I might say "snake", something I loathed and feared thanks in part to Daddy's water skiing story.

"Maybe we should go home," I told Philip, meaning Newitville, not San Francisco.

"There's nothing we can do right now that we can't do from the phone."

After the rain stopped, we walked from the park back to the French Quarter, it took about an hour and when we reached Canal Street, it started to rain again. We ducked into a dive bar and drank a couple of bottles of Dixie beer, we sat next to the door and watched the rain. I thought odd details about Daddy, like how in the seventies he had two leisure suits, one light blue, one forest green. He wore a yellow clip-on tie with both. And a short sleeve white shirt because he didn't want to bother with cuffs. He wore the suits only on Friday nights when he took Mama and me to Fortunato's, his favorite restaurant. A blind organist played songs from the forties while we ate Steak Diane and Oysters Rockefeller and my parents drank highballs.

And I also thought about how my father worked his jaw when he was mad, and how dandruff fell on the shoulders of his blue flannel jacket in the winter, and his strange theory that clothes worked together if they were colors found in nature. Hence, he'd pair orange and forest green, or rust and gold, the colors of fall, and lighter shades of green and blue and yellow, spring colors.

The funny thing is, as we sat in the bar drinking beer, I didn't think about the things that defined my father, like his love of Ole Miss Rebels football, or Frank Sinatra's music, or drinking, or reading *Civil War Times*. Over the course of my life, if you picked out any random moment, there is a ninety percent chance he would be doing one of those things. Instead, I thought mainly about the clothes he wore. Maybe it was just easier, some sort of grief mechanism kicking in, helping me deal with the course of the next few weeks.

A woman in Georgia caught AIDS from a pay phone. She was a good Baptist, a grandmother who paid her taxes and voted Republican in every election. She didn't drink or smoke, and her friends said she had not had sex in twelve years — since her husband died. There had been a spot of blood on the receiver, which she hadn't noticed until she hung up and saw the red smeared on her palm.

The same thing happened to a grandmother in Northern Florida and another in South Carolina. It happened to a church friend of Aunt Pie's neighbor's sister's co-worker.

Judging by the number of people who knew someone afflicted by AIDS from a phone booth, it happened to a quarter of the Southern female senior citizen population.

Daddy had once sent me a clipping from a tabloid that described one such ordeal. He scrawled at the top of the article, "Be careful out there in Frisco with all them fairies!"

The rain let up and Philip and I left the bar. As soon as we got to our hotel room, I called Dr. Kelly again.

"Are you sure we don't need a second opinion?" I asked. He was sure, though he said that was entirely my option.

"And we really can't operate?"

"We really can't. It would do no good, only harm."

"How did this happen?" I asked.

"How does any disease happen? Your father drank a lot, he didn't exercise or eat particularly well. Environment has something to do with it, fate is all the rest."

Philip and I spent three days in New Orleans. Our largest expense was the phone bill. I called Newitville often, talking to Dr. Kelly, or my mother, who was in denial and told me a total of twenty-seven times (I counted) that Daddy had beat cancer before, remember? Hell, he beat colon cancer!

"Hell, he'll beat it again," she said one more time, with the vigor of a steer.

I spoke a few times to Daddy, who sounded cheery, and agreed with my mother that he'd "lick this thing." Nothing revved them up like a good battle. It appealed to the Rebel aspect in my father, meaning the Ole Miss Rebels. Archie Manning, the star quarterback of the best Rebels team ever, may as well have been facing down the fourth down in the fourth quarter of a losing game against the LSU Tigers. Archie would win — he always did — and so would Daddy! Why? Because he and Mama had team spirit. They sounded like a pep squad facing off Cancer for the Rebel homecoming.

"It's just a disease. These days, it's like the flu," Mama actually said.

"Hell, really, the flu is a bigger threat to me than cancer," Daddy said. "I mean, I can get radiation for cancer."

In one conversation, I told my father what Dr. Kelly said about Mama having to go into a home.

"Shit!" he said. "That ain't good. I guess you might as well find two beds. Because I'm going with her."

"That's the other thing Dr. Kelly said," I told him. In our last call he told me that my father couldn't continue to stay in the hospital, and he, too, needed nursing care. A home would suit him better, as his condition, though terminal, was ironically not critical.

"Shit," Daddy said again.

I only remember snippets of the pleasurable part of our New Orleans' trip. We ate beignets at Café DuMond and split a muffaletta at Central Grocery. We swam in bottles of Dixie Beer and shopped at Jackson Square. We watched the street artists perform along the sidewalks and one afternoon, I opened the doors to our balcony at the Richelieu and watched the rain splat down on the large magnolia tree across the street. Its blossoms, big as pasta bowls, looked like globs of snow against the dark green leaves, which were as wide as canoe paddles.

The air smelled a mixture of sweet olive blossom and beer vomit; the thunder reminded me of my childhood, when every summer afternoon ended in a brief rainstorm. I stood there a long time while Philip napped and I wondered why I felt so numb, why I wasn't a wreck and why I didn't cry. I didn't know what the appropriate emotion was supposed to be. If my life were a made-for-television movie, I'd be on my knees breaking down.

But I just didn't feel anything, yet my brain kept moving like an old movie reel, clacking over old family images. I saw my mother in her horn-rimmed glasses from the 1960s, I saw JFK Jr. in his little coat on television, saluting his father's coffin, and I heard Daddy say, "Now that's a damn sad sight." I saw Grandma sitting in her rocking chair crocheting while we watched the lunar landing on television. I could hear Grandpa's hoary voice calling my name and Daddy singing off key to Sinatra's "Summer Wind." I could taste my parent's Jack Daniel's and ginger ale over melting ice, and smell the pungent aroma of crawfish boiling in a bouquet of spices on the kitchen stove.

The rain stopped and the leaves from and the building gutters dripped water. The hot, moist air from the Mississippi River swept over the street and I still stood there, thinking of all these strange things from my past.

During the late seventies/early eighties or maybe the mid-nineties, two young lovers had been forbidden by the girl's parents to see each other anymore. So they stuck an eight-track, or a cassette, or a CD of Leonard Skynard's "Freebird" into the car stereo and drove their Trans Am into a brick wall. Actually, they may have played "Stairway to Heaven" or "Sweet Home Alabama." I've heard this story many times and the song is always different.

Daddy hated rock and roll. He called it "Yeah, Yeah" music. The first song I remember ever hearing was Sinatra's "All or Nothing at All." My mother used to sing it to me at night to help me go to sleep. She had a sweet voice, but the older she got, the more it cracked and popped like a worn record.

She and Daddy called the Rat Pack's songs, "their music." By that they meant their generation's music. But in my mind, Frank and Dean's songs were created just for my parents. Sinatra, in particular, sang the sound tracks to our life. There was "Summer Wind," for all those summers I spent at home growing up, playing amidst the old cedars and pines in the woods behind our house. I dodged snakes and dug the earth for Civil War mini-balls, or played hide and seek (me hiding) with Dino Martin, the fat spotted mongrel.

"In the Wee Small Hours," summed up the nights Ava came home late from dates and my parents sat up, worried, biting their nails because she had proven time and again to have horrific tastes taste in men. She preferred ones with unemployment checks in their back pockets, or DUI's stuffed in their dresser drawer.

And then there was "High Hopes," a perpetual state of being for me and my parents. We had high hopes we would somehow come into money and be able to move out of our rundown house and buy something bigger and better.

Three weeks after returning to San Francisco, I flew back to Mississippi to settle affairs. I had found a nursing home for Mama and Daddy, but the space wouldn't be available for a few weeks, and in the meantime, I needed to sell their house and the furniture. They could only take the essential things they wanted and needed, plus a few personal items.

Ava kept sending emails saying, "Hey, if there's anything I can do, let me know." There was plenty she could do, but with children she couldn't just drop everything and come down. So I did it all, mainly because I truly didn't know what to delegate. It was just easier to do it myself.

Reality had begun to sink in for my father. Mama was still in happy denial. Maybe her brain had deteriorated so much that she could not comprehend the truth, that her husband of forty-nine years was about to die. "I hope he lives long enough so we can celebrate our fiftieth anniversary," she told me on my first day there.

She wanted to ride around town with me while I did all my errands. She was only sixty-eight, but she looked and acted eighty. Her skin was like rice paper, thin, crackly. She walked with a cane.

We had been driving around all morning, running to various bureaucratic offices, like the veterans' administration, Medicare, and social security. We waited in long lines with people visibly poor, some, clearly destitute, a word the woman at Medicare used to describe my parents situation. The nursing home would cost $32,000 a year per parent. VA would cover Daddy. Mama had to apply for

Medicaid, which she qualified for, as soon as we sold the house and applied all her equity toward the nursing home. Philip and I could not afford to help her, even if we changed our lifestyle, which was not that extravagant.

We had to go to the courthouse to get a copy of the deed to their property because Mama couldn't find her copy. It was an unusually hot day, even for Mississippi in the dead of summer. As we climbed the stairs, Mama had one of her dizzy spells, an after-affect of the strokes. She wobbled and I grabbed her. It was a moment when I could have shown some compassion, but I lost my temper.

"God-damnit, this wouldn't have happened if you hadn't drank all these years," I said. I had her by the elbow and was slowly pulling her along.

"I know it, I know it." She sounded ready to cry, but her eyes were dry.

"Daddy's in the mess he's in because of Jack Daniel's, too."

"I hear you."

"I begged you two to stop. I told you that you all had a problem, but you didn't listen to me."

"You don't know what our lives were like."

"You don't know what mine was like because of yours."

We got to the top of the stairs and I stopped. My mother was panting and I got this image of joggers in Golden Gate Park, holding the end of a leash while their dog ran to keep up. I had always considered it cruel.

"I know you are scared and that's why you are mad at me. But your daddy will pull through, don't worry," she said, breathless.

I held onto her elbow tighter and looked her in the eyes so there would be no mistaking my words. "No, he won't. We have to get used to that."

"I know it," she said, and laughed lightly. I led her into the cool courthouse and took her over to a bench and told her to wait for me. While I dealt with a clerk who couldn't understand how someone could lose their copy of a property deed, which Mama had done with a good bit of ease, I could see my mother out of the corner of my eye. She sat staring into the cold air. I wondered what she thought, her neurons sputtering and misfiring in her stroke-smoothed mind.

Two sisters once lost their parents when their airplane plummeted into Lake Charles. One of the sisters, the older one, was supposed to be on the plane with them; they were going to visit the younger sister. At the last minute, the older sister got overwhelming images of her death. She begged her parents not to get on the plane. They laughed off her fears. She stayed behind.

After the funeral, the sisters put aside their grief to fight over their parents' estate. In particular, they argued over the toaster, which had been in the family since they were kids. It still worked, and they thought it must surely be worth something. As it turned out, the mother had inadvertently promised it to them both. They couldn't agree on who should get it, and neither wanted to split the profits. Things got so out of control that the younger sister killed the older sister by knocking her over the head with the toaster. The older sister had not foreseen her own death.

Ava told me that story once, joking that there would be very few items of worth for us to argue over once our parents were gone. At the end of my long day of running around town to all the bureaucratic offices, I called Ava and told her the news about selling the house and the nursing home. "There goes my inheritance," she said. "We can't have any money for ourselves?"

For a moment, I couldn't say anything. I was trying to determine if she was serious or not. Then she said, "This is just like them isn't it?" and I knew she was not joking.

"You're welcome to anything in the house, Ava. They can't take the furniture and stuff with them, just some clothes and a few knickknacks for their dresser."

She made a noise that sounded like a cross between a guffaw and a harrumph and in general expressed succinctly her deep dissatisfaction.

"Maybe you want their toaster," I said, thinking of the story she had told me.

"Why would I want that piece of shit?" she said. "What I would like is some money. I have bills to pay, you know."

"There isn't any money for us."

She sighed, deeper than anyone in history has ever sighed. "Well, other than that, how are you?"

"Oh, I'm just great," I said, biting off the words so she would notice my sarcasm. "Just great."

She didn't notice my tone. "Oh that's good."

A man and his mother and wife were once out for a Sunday drive in the country. The man suddenly pulled over and started walking through the woods to a clearing where a monument marked a Civil War battle. "This is where Great, Great Uncle Harris fought and died," he declared."

"How do you know?" his wife asked. "Have you been to this battlefield before?"

"I know because I was there." He began telling the women how he remembered sitting up against a tall oak, which he pointed out. It had been a clear, crisp winter day. "December," he said. He had been wounded in the belly. He could vaguely remember his gray wool uniform. The sleeves were too short. The jacket itched and was damp from having been rained on the day before. The man and women read the marker and it turned out that he was correct about the battle that he said had been fought there.

"But how could you know this?" his mother asked.

"I know. I can't explain it, but I was there."

That man was my father. I thought about this story often now, and the possibility of reincarnation. I marveled that a man who called homosexuals "fairies" and Japanese "nips," who confused football with religion and considered television dramas high culture, could so whole-heartedly believe in a Buddhist concept like reincarnation. But I never saw my father more serious than the few times he talked about his vivid memories from another life. He didn't like to discuss it, though it did lend to his belief that he was truly a Civil War authority since he had actually been there.

I stayed at Aunt Teckla's house during my time in Newitville. My parents' home was a hopeless wreck. In the months leading up to my father's illness, they had let things go more than usual. They had a housekeeper who came out a couple of times a month, but she got tired of the mess my mother seemed to create after each visit and quit. There were piles and piles of dirty clothes everywhere. In my old bedroom, on their bedroom floor, on living room chairs. There were large bags full of garbage they had not taken outside. Magazines and mail piled the kitchen table and their dressers. They had not swept. Dirty dishes filled the sink and spilled onto the counters. Every item in the refrigerator needed to be thrown out.

But there was more. The roof leaked and the water damage had created holes in the ceiling. Once, a pack of rats lived in the attic. But now, even they had moved out.

Teckla and I tried to clean up, but we couldn't fight our fear that every time we opened a door or cabinet, a snake would leap out and kill us. We cleaned for six hours, though, and barely made a dent. We filled up nearly thirty large bags of garbage and made two trips in my father's truck to the county dump. By the end of the day, the stench of garbage was so permeated in my skin that I could not escape the odor. I thought my nostrils had been damaged permanently. I felt horrible, loathsome, that as their daughter, I had let their lives deteriorate like this.

"You're living out in California," Teckla said. "You couldn't have known it was this bad." If I didn't know how bad it had gotten, I knew it had a starting point. I had stopped coming to the house years earlier in a tough-love protest. Drinking had caused both of my parents to get slothful. I tired quickly of dirty floors, grimy tubs, moldy food in the refrigerator, and having to wash a glass every time I wanted a drink of water. I always stayed at Teckla's. My parents, I think, were relieved. They didn't have to go through the pretense of cleaning.

I should have known it had gotten worse. I kept sending money for housekeepers, but they always quit. Mama's response was, "It's just hard to find good help." Seeing the house now, I think the women were overwhelmed by the task at hand.

Still, I defended myself by saying, "I didn't know it was this bad. Mama was always telling me how good the house looked now. She said she had cleaned it up herself."

"Your mama likes to invent her own truths. I've never known anyone who makes things up the way she does."

The next morning, I brought a friend of my parents' out to the house, a real estate agent, George Hinkle. He took one look around and sniffed.

"Sugar," George said, "this sad ass *thang* should be condemned. I can get you maybe $15,000, but that's just for the property. With this damn fire-trap, you should pay someone to take it off your hands."

The rest of my week in Newitville is a blur of errands. I filled up the tank in Aunt Teckla's car twice. I slept hard and deep. Since I agreed with George's assessment of my parent's house, both Mama and I stayed at Teckla's. The three of us would go into the den at eight o'clock each night and watch their favorite shows, things like "Touched by an Angel" or reruns of "In the Heat of the Night" or "Murder She Wrote." The kind of television that AARP would endorse.

I visited Daddy in the hospital between chores. He always had the television on, and oddly enough, no matter what time of the day, either reruns of "Touched by an Angel," "In the Heat of the Night," or "Murder She Wrote," were on. I began to think these were the only programs shown in Mississippi.

At one point, during a fight with Ava over the phone, I finally cried. She was complaining about how our parents pissed away all their money and I said that they never had any real money. We never went without clothes when we needed them, but that was because Mama and Daddy ran up excessive debt. I had their $10,000 Visa bill in my hands to prove it.

"I'm not paying off their debt," Ava said.

"You don't have to," I said. "I can use the money from the sale of the house. I can spend all the money, as long as it's spent on Mama. That's the only way Medicaid will pay for her nursing home."

"I'm just so mad that they didn't think about us more."

And that's when I lost it. I started crying and whimpering how "I couldn't take it anymore." I said things I had heard Mama say over the years, like "I do and I do for this family and I get no thanks in return."

Ava hung up. I hung up. Aunt Teckla came into the room, saw me, and started crying, too. I said, "This is too much."

"This is too much for me, too," she said.

"I feel like everything is on me."

"I feel like I'm in the center of it all," she cried. And she was. We had turned her house into crisis central, sleeping there, using her phone. In the weeks before, while I was in California, she had carried the burden of schlepping my mother around, running her errands, dealing with the hospital.

Teckla grabbed a box of tissues off the top of her bookshelf and we sat next to each other dabbing our eyes.

There are countless stories about loved ones saying goodbye to a loved one who is going to the grocery store for a six-pack of beer or soda, or a carton of milk or cigarettes. As the door shuts, the beloved left in the house is swept over with a cold feeling that they will never see that person again. And sure enough, their son, daughter, husband, mother, father, or wife, whoever it was that got in the car to go to the store, is hit head on by a big rig, just two blocks from their home, and killed instantly.

At the end of the week, I had finished most of the details of closing down my father's life. My own life waited for me in California. My husband was lonely, my boss was a mess because she was short staffed and had to pick up the slack. My cats, Sammy Davis and Liza Minnelli, were turning wild, pacing, yowling, knowing instinctively that their world was a little off because one of their owners was not around. There was one less human feeding and loving them and they didn't like that. They left little gifts for Philip on our bed, gifts wrapped in kitty litter. He patiently cleaned up after them and then would hold them for hours at a time, petting them till they purred with security. But after he went to sleep, they would revert back to their ways, scratching furniture; yowling in the middle of the night as if they were being slaughtered.

They basically acted out the things I wished I could get away with.

I had to go home. I told myself I would come back to Mississippi in a few weeks, I told my mother and father and Teckla the same. But a little voice in my head whispered, "Na-uh. You won't be back till the funeral." Fear, large and dark, nudged at my conscience. I could handle bureaucrats with their long lines and their numbing forms. I excelled at the details, but when it came down to that moment where I had to look my father in the eyes and talk about his future, I choked. Fright swept over me, a curtain blocking out the unforeseen and keeping it silent.

This is how I spent the last hour I ever had with my father: He lay in his bed and we watched in the "Heat of the Night" on the television that hung high on the wall across from his bed. I had never watched the show, though it was his favorite. In the seventies I had wanted to watch Carroll O'Connor's other show, "All in the Family." Daddy wouldn't let me. He didn't like its liberal agenda. Thirty years later, we're watching the same star play a sheriff from Mississippi. It was a repeat. Daddy didn't watch new episodes, because O'Connor's character had married a black woman. Daddy wasn't comfortable with that.

Even facing death, some people never change. In an odd, unfortunate way, I found this comforting. Daddy was staying true to his course till the end.

We didn't talk much, unless it was to comment on the show. I sat there and stared at the screen and thought about death, and how I'd always feared my parents' dying, just like any kid did. I had thought about it a thousand times over the years, wondering about it. How would it happen, what would it be like, how would I handle it? As I sat there, closer to the momentous event than ever before, I thought, "I don't know I don't know I don't know."

And then I thought, "I'm too young to lose a parent."

I felt strong, alone, weak, loved, and needed.

When the show ended, I looked at my watch and knew it was time to go to Jackson. I had a plane to catch. I gave an obligatory sigh, the kind people give when they are reluctant to admit that they need to leave. Daddy said, "Is it time?" and I said, "yes."

Mama slept in a chair near the window. She did much of that these days.

Daddy said, "Don't wake her, it's easier this way."

I didn't quite know what he meant, and I was too scared to ask, scared like the kind of scared actors in movies pretend like they feel, so scared, you, in the audience, are supposed to feel it, too. But you can't, not till you've been in that moment. And then, then you know what scared is really all about and there are no words to do it justice.

I kissed Daddy goodbye on the forehead. It was a quick kiss and I can still feel the touch of his skin on my lips, hot and clammy at once. This disease defied all odds. A stray hair above his lip, so gray it was almost invisible, pricked me.

He told me he loved me and I said I loved him too. It was not a comfortable moment, telling each other we loved each other was never comfortable. We acted like we were embarrassed to admit it, that we were chagrined to admit fondness for anyone, even each other.

I walked out of the room and told myself not to look back, that if I looked back, I'd cry or he'd cry and we didn't need that. We needed to be strong. It was the only way either of us would feel comfortable.

I walked down the hallway to the elevator. There was a black family already in the car, a mother with her little girl and boy. The doors were about to close and I stuck my hand in so I could get on. They glared at me silently. The little girl stuck her thumb in her mouth and laid her head against her mother's leg, who put a protective arm around the child. I felt radioactive and bad, and it occurred to me, I was witnessing and inadvertently participating in the poor race relations I had always sworn really didn't take place in Mississippi.

And I thought, Shit, it's just one more thing.

A father dies, or a mother, a son, a daughter, a best friend, or even a pet. They are all variations of the same story. At the same time as the loved one dies, someone close to that person feels the loss immediately, even though they are 100 miles away, 1000 miles away or 3,000 miles away.

For me, nothing happened. A few weeks after returning from Mississippi, I had just come home from work and the phone rang. It was Aunt Teckla saying that Daddy had just died. I had tried to talk to him the day before when I called, but Mama had answered and said he didn't feel well. He wasn't saying much. She asked if he wanted to speak to me and he shook his head no. The next day, his breathing became erratic and he was rushed to the hospital.

He died alone in intensive care. Mama and Teckla had gone downstairs to find the doctor and get some more information before they called me and Ava. I've heard stories like that before, where the wife, or husband or child leaves the hospital room for just a moment and the loved one dies. A nurse saw his monitor flat lining. She came into his room and he was gone.

I wonder now if he knew he didn't have much longer, and by not taking my call avoided having to say goodbye. I try to imagine him in those last moments, like the twilight between asleep and awake and I wonder what he was thinking. He had told me in Vegas that his happiest years were when Ava and I were growing up. Did he think about those days then, or did he wonder what was ahead, blackness or light? Maybe he thought he would soon see the loved ones he'd lost, his mother and father, his daughter Janice from his first marriage. Or even some of his Civil War buddies, from his last life.

I hope he wasn't scared, I hope he wasn't aware that this was It and that he was Alone. A friend later told me that it was a tragedy I wasn't there at his side to say goodbye. I've often heard stories of people by the side of their loved ones, saying goodbye. I never understood it. How can you say goodbye adequately? It's a fruitless attempt at making things better. There are no words to express a lifetime.

There are other death stories, all involving the last time you kiss a loved one on the forehead, the final time they hear you tell them you love them, the words they utter before passing on. In some stories there is a death rattle, in some a strange, cool breeze. In every one, however, there is sadness and heartache. But none describe the gaping hole that exists at your core after the loved one shuts his or her eyes and lets out that very last breath. Come to think of it, I can't recall any stories that ever talk about that.

Chapter Fourteen
Your Light, My Shadow

After Daddy died, I started to resent my mother even more. She needed my frequent attention. Other than Teckla, there was no one else to give her any. Pie was relishing her old age and pension fund by gambling, drinking and smoking daily at one of the riverboat casinos outside Newitville. Ava lived somewhere in the South. I had lost track she moved and married or shacked up so often.

The nursing home took care of Mama's day-to-day needs, but it was Teckla and I who visited her (Teckla more often than me as she lived in Newitville). I called weekly, sometimes several times. I flew home more often now, four or five times a year. My visits were still short. My mother was barely seventy and she was in this bad shape because she drank so hard for so many years.

And then it all ended rather abruptly two years after Daddy died. In the days that followed my mother's death, I half-jokingly told a few friends that I had become an expert on family death. "I'm orphaned at 37," I told them, trying to make light of it all.

The people I wanted to get away from had gotten away from it all, permanently, with Mama holding up the withered rank. She passed away during the early hours the morning after Christmas. A light snow fell in Newitville. Aunt Teckla said as she went to bed that night, she looked out the window and saw the flakes falling, so pretty and peaceful. "You know, it never snows at Christmas, and I thought to myself, God is blessing us tonight. It was so damn pretty."

The nursing home called Teckla just after midnight and told her that an ambulance had taken Mama to the hospital. The night nurse found her lying in bed, her head cocked to the side like she had been looking at the snow fall outside her window.

I had spoken to Mama just that morning. I felt bad for not being there, but Philip hated flying during the holiday rush, and frankly, I hated spending holidays in Newitville, so I used his distaste for travel as an excuse. But I'd called Mama to wish her a Merry Christmas. Her voice sounded foggy and she lisped because her teeth were "soaking next to her bed." It is one of the few things she told me in our short conversation. I pictured them sitting in a glass of water on her nightstand, the fillings shining like jewels in a deep-sea treasure chest.

Mama said, "My stomach hurts."

"Oh, I'm sorry," I said, unnaturally sweet compared to my usual tone with her, I'm ashamed to admit. The older we both got, the more she wore down my nerves. She repeated herself often and cut me off when I was speaking, taking the conversation in a completely different direction.

But this Christmas, for some reason, I felt patient and well, full of kindness.

"Do you have big plans today, Mama?" I cooed. I had taken to talking to her like she was a child. That's how people spoke to the folks in the nursing home and I picked up the habit.

"Hmmph. Here," she said and handed the phone to Aunt Teckla, who was visiting with gifts.

"She's not feeling well," Teckla told me, then she said in half-whisper, "She's awfully cranky. But I can tell she loves the slippers and robe you sent. They're so soft! And what a pretty purple! She's got them on right now, don't you sugar?" she said to Mama. I could hear Mama grunt back.

We hung up a few moments later and I felt relief that I was going to escape a Christmas without Mama making me feel guilty about not moving back home.

Then, around one o'clock the next morning, the phone rang, and it was Teckla, telling me Mama had a stomach aneurysm and was gone.

I said, "Awww." I realized immediately that a whiney "awww" was a very inappropriate response. I said, "Aneurysm . . . in the stomach?"

"In the stomach. It burst."

"You can get an aneurysm in the stomach?"

"I guess so."

"And her aneurysm just burst?"

"It burst. It sure did."

"That's an odd way to die." We talked a minute longer about how we'd get some sleep and talk more later in the morning. But before hanging up, she said, "You know, I waited to call you sugar. I waited till after midnight your time because I didn't want your Christmas to be ruined."

"Aunt Teckla, I think it's already ruined," I told her. Then I said, "I love you, Aunt Teckla." And she said, "I love you, Lisa Tingle Dubois."

Philip slept next to me; the ringing phone had not interrupted his rest. I hung up and lay in the darkness. I felt nothing, or to be precise, I felt numb. Then something strange happened. My mother visited me.

At first, I just felt her. The cold room turned warm. I had this mental image of her better than she was in life. A light radiated from her and I pictured her as whole, emotionally that is. The feeling grew stronger and then, there she was, standing at the edge of my bed wearing a flowing white garb and glowing from within. She smiled serenely at me. I sat up in bed to talk to her, and the next thing that happened is . . . it was morning and I was waking up.

I stayed in bed awhile, remembering this odd occurrence. The happiness and peace I had felt at seeing her diminished. I finally started to cry. They were the kind of tears my mother shed when she had too much to drink and the hurts in her life overwhelmed her: hard crying, an expulsion of deep-down hurt. Her tears had always pushed me away and left me cold toward her; I never understood why she cried so often.

Grief set in, full-blown and black. I couldn't stop crying to plan the funeral. Aunt Teckla and Pie did all the work. Not that there was much to do. Mama was to be cremated. I had bought her urn two years earlier with my father's. Years ago, they had selected four plots in the cemetery. Their own, and one for me and one for Ava.

So all that was left for my aunts to do was call the Reverend down at Christ Episcopal Church, the funeral home, the relatives, and the *Newitville Evening Post*. The nursing home took care of social security and Medicaid.

I cried all day. I cried so much Philip got to the point where he didn't even attempt to console me anymore. So he called all my friends and told them what had happened.

My crying eased by the time I woke on the second day after she died, and I decided all of a sudden to become a Buddhist. It was one of those odd decisions people make to get through a rough time. Mama's spirit had visited me and she was now well on her way to being somebody else. Her soul had another chance. My friends were amazed at how well I handled her death. They called me a "beacon of strength," a "tower of will." I had been down for a day but, damn, did I bounce back better than ever.

Phillip and I flew to Mississippi. We rented a Cadillac (he thought, given the circumstances, I should drive something nice) and drove to Aunt Teckla's house. Ava was already there, with her latest husband, Conner. They drove up from New Orleans where they lived. Ava had worked for Conner. He was a lawyer at the time, but had since been disbarred. Ava would never tell us why, only that it was a "long story" that involved a "ruthless bitch."

Lucy and JW did not come with her.

I asked Ava where they were.

She waved a hand like it was nothing. "I told them, Hell, Grandma's dead. She don't care if you come or not. Believe you me."

Monica flew in from Utah for Mama's funeral. She worked as a fashion writer in New York. She had been visiting Mr. Priestly and his wife, who were skiing near Salt Lake.

Monica sat at my aunt's table and chain-smoked. She did not say much, except to make the occasional witty comment. Of particular note, she made a jab at Mississippi's educational system, "or rather, the lack of it," as she said. I thought she was funny, and, in fact, was a great source of comic relief. Well, at least to me she was.

The others at the table did not find her so amusing. Pie and Teckla turned red with each well-oiled verbal jab. And then there was cousin Bitty who had driven up from New Orleans. She took Monica's insults about Mississippi as an injury against the South. Bitty still hadn't gotten over the fact that Jimmy Carter not only lost the 1980 election, but that the South had voted against him. "It is simply reprehensible behavior," she'd say. "People forget who they are."

The evening would have continued without rancor were it not for an unfortunate recent tragedy in Pearl, Mississippi, which I made the mistake of mentioning. A teenage boy went on a shooting rampage at his school.

Bitty spoke in a confidential tone about the matter. "Well, you know, they say he worshipped Satan."

This provoked a response from Monica. "He didn't worship Satan. He was just a screwed up kid with a gun."

"Well, no, he was a Satan worshipper. Satan made him pull the trigger."

"The kid's parents had an arsenal in their house. He pulled the trigger. That's all there is to it."

"Well, it's a tragedy."

"It's a tragedy yes, but people are animals and as long as we have guns, we have killings. We need tighter gun control."

"If you don't have guns, you don't have freedom," Bitty said.

"Please."

"No guns, no freedom."

And so on. They went at it. Bitty kept repeating "No guns, No freedom" and Monica hammered her with statistics about countries with tight gun control laws and low crime. Bitty pushed herself up from the table and left, slamming the door behind her so hard the house shook. Teckla gave me the evil eye, a warning that Monica, my friend, therefore my responsibility, had outworn her welcome.

Ava, at an attempt to break the tension, made this unfortunate comment: "You know, I don't like guns either, Monica. My third husband once shoved a pistol down my throat and told me if I didn't have sex with him, he'd kill me."

Monica said, *"Nice."*

The death rays from Aunt Teckla's evil eye got hotter.

Since Teckla's house was full with Bitty and Ava and them, Philip, Monica and I stayed at the Holiday Inn on Lee Street. Monica had an adjoining room next to ours. Philip went to bed at his usual time, ten o'clock, and Monica and I stayed up in her room, watching David Letterman and talking very little. We had been friends for over thirty years, there wasn't much to say that we had not already said.

"You okay?" she asked me after a while.

"My mother's dead. I feel really bad actually."

She took a long drag on her cigarette then exhaled the smoke slowly, the plume, fat and elegant, the feat only an experienced smoker can achieve. "You don't choose your family."

"I know."

"You aren't your family."

"Mmm."

"It's okay to feel relief."

I looked at her. "Relief?"

"Isn't that what you feel?"

I had to think about it. With each of my relatives' deaths, I never really understood what I felt, except a depthless feeling of loss. A deep hole where something in the center of me had once been. Not much anger. A lot of regret. General sadness. But I was always okay, so okay that I felt bad. My reaction was the opposite of others I knew. I knew people who couldn't get over a parent's death. It ruined them. Me? I took each loss like a bad flu. In two weeks I bounced back. Maybe I was quiet for a while, and distracted. As I thought about it, that's the word that summed up how I felt: distracted. Purposely distracted.

I turned back to Letterman. He was doing his dumb redneck imitation, saying, "Duh," like he did. I wasn't listening. Monica said something. I didn't hear. I was thinking about the way Mama laughed, the way her eyes teared up when she laughed hard, the way her belly and jowls jiggled. It was my favorite thing about her. I could make her laugh like no one. Every time she laughed, I felt as if I had saved the world.

Mama did not have a large turnout for her funeral, maybe forty people. Many were friends of Teckla and Pie who had come to lend support to them. Few people from the church came, and even fewer from the nursing home, mainly because they were too feeble.

It was the lack of relatives that I noticed. That stung hard. Even some of the younger ones were gone. Quinn had died of lung cancer, just like his father before I was born. Carson had also passed away. One winter night, about a year after Quinn had gone, Carson drove to a favorite spot of hers, overlooking the Mississippi River. She lived outside New Orleans, in a swampy area where there were few people. A romantic, she liked the evocative mystery of the area, with its twisted, gnarled Cyprus and Spanish moss.

She liked to drive to this spot and watch the sun set through the swamp. She had told me many times, that the light was true amber, warm. "It's sent straight from God," she would say.

It had been raining in previous days, and her car got stuck in the soft, muddy shoulder of the road where she had parked. To keep warm, she kept the engine running with the heat on, till someone drove by. No one did, not for hours. By that time, she had died of carbon monoxide poisoning, as the cars tailpipe had sunk deep in the mud.

On the day of Mama's funeral I felt the loss of them and all my relatives. Even the ones who weren't dead, but had scattered to the far points of the South. Especially my remaining cousins, who seldom made it back to Newitville; it would take more than my mother's funeral to drag them back. Other than Bitty, none of the New Orleans' relatives came — and they didn't know her well enough for her to ever piss them off. The funeral was simply another reminder that my mother had been a difficult person to love.

Lester now lived in South Beach, in Miami. Delia lived in Mobile. Her life revolved around the factory where she worked as a secretary, and her holy roller church, Jesus of Nazareth. Then there was mean-as-a-water-moccasin cousin Van. He now lived in Georgia, in the kind of town that sprang up around a truck stop. He worked at odd jobs and through a miracle, had never been to jail. It didn't bother me that he did not return for the funeral.

The relatives that did come to the funeral partook in a ritual Carson had once labeled as "Adults Behaving Badly." Before the service, as people gathered in the recreation room downstairs in the church, Pie took me aside and said, "That Monica is a stinker."

Aunt Teckla was right behind her, her gray hair perfectly coifed. She smelled of Heaven Scent, and held an unlit cigarette between two fingers.

"She is not welcome in my house anymore." Teckla stuck the cigarette in her lips and sucked hard as if she might actually draw in smoke. She had given up smoking six months earlier. Sucking on the unlit cigarette made her feel better.

Then Bitty walked up, tears flowing with a velocity that matched Teckla's ire, and said, "I cannot believe you cremated your mother." She buried her red nose in a pink handkerchief and let the sobs rip.

"I really don't think Monica meant to offend anyone," I said to Teckla and Pie. I didn't know what to say to Bitty

"Doesn't she know I'm grieving?" Teckla said. "I just lost my little sister."

"Oh forget Monica. I can't believe Lisa cremated Belle," Cousin Bitty sobbed.

"Monica is a stinker," Aunt Pie repeated.

"My mother died," I said, in answer to all three. "And at least Monica is here to pay her respects which is more than I can say for your children."

I walked away, knowing they were madder at me than ever, and no doubt, discussing at length what a stinker I had become.

A volume of tears spouted as soon as I walked into the church. Mama-like tears, unabashed, aimless. I was surprised at how much I felt the loss of Mama. I was surprised at how bad regret hurt, and I knew this pain was more regret than loss. I mourned for that hole in my heart, the one full of grief for the close relationship I wanted — had she been sober.

And I cried, too, because I felt awful for Mama. Even her death elicited vexation. It was like the person had died, but the aggravation lived on.

I bent my head over and Philip, who had been invisible to me with all the arguing and hurt feelings since we had arrived, put his arm around me. I whispered in his ear, "I have no family anymore, not really." And he whispered back in my ear, "With family like you've got, who needs enemies?"

I had just reached the point where I could focus on the pastor's words and stop crying when I noticed the nativity table on the other side of the front row of pews. The small figurines were the size of a large man's fingers. They were yellowed and cracked and looked only slightly less pathetic than the wilted poinsettias framing the altar stairs. I had wanted white roses, but the church had a rule, that dictated we must use the flowers and plants already in the church, hence, the poinsettias.

There was no music because the organist had the flu. So on top of all the tackiness, we had only the sound of the Reverend's somber voice and the unsettled shuffling of the congregation.

I felt like a character in a Truman Capote short story, replete with his famous distaste for the lowly poinsettias. But it would have been a story Truman would have trashed, thinking, "No one's funeral could be that God awful."

If I found any shred of relief in the ceremony, Ava erased it soon afterwards. I had asked her to ride with Philip and me to the cemetery. As she closed the door to the back seat, she said casually, without any feeling, "You know, Lisa, I don't know why you are crying. I always thought Mama was a pig."

That night, I dreamt of my mother and my father and my grandparents. We were in the kitchen of my family's home, sitting around the table, which was covered with newspaper and a pile of boiled crawfish. We laughed and talked and I had this incredible feeling that I was loved, entirely, that I could do no wrong in these people's eyes. Though they had their disagreements, it didn't change the way they felt about me, and as long as I could remember that, I would be okay.

When I woke up the next morning, I understood what the dream meant. With the exception of Philip, all the people who loved me most had died. I had always wanted *tabula rasa* in my life, a blank slate to start over. With my mother's death, I had been handed the slate. I felt the full impact of Jean Paul Sartre's line, "We are condemned to be free." Freedom had bitch-slapped me, and I stung with fear and loneliness.

As if to prove my point, Monica left Newitville that day. She had an assignment in Paris to cover a new up and coming designer who was supposed to be more brilliant than the latest new up and coming brilliant designer. She would go to Paris, the jet-setting dream of our youth now a part of her ordinary work schedule. I would return to chilly San Francisco and write drab proposals for drab projects.

After seeing Monica off, I left the hotel and returned to Teckla's. It was our last day in Newitville and despite how things were at the funeral, I felt I should spend some time with them and say good-bye, especially since I did not know when, or if, I would ever return to Newitville.

As soon as I arrived, Cousin Bitty took me aside before she left to go back to New Orleans. "I just want you to know," she said in a quiet confidential voice, "I am appalled that you cremated your mother. That is just not right."

Teckla and Pie stepped in before I could respond. "Did that stinker Monica leave yet?" Pie asked.

I nodded.

"Good," Bitty said. "She has the manners of a horse."

"She has no right coming down here and telling us how we should live our lives," Teckla said.

"She's a stinker," Pie said.

"She wasn't that bad. What's wrong with a little lively debate? Come on. She's my best friend," I said.

"Your best friend is a stinker," Pie said, and lit up a Pall Mall.

The next morning Philip and I woke early to catch a flight home. We dressed, packed the suitcase we shared for the trip and loaded up the car, shivering in the front seat waiting for the windshield to defrost. My mind was blank, pleasantly so, as if amnesia had swept over me during my sleep. I had dreamt of my loved ones again, the ones who had passed away. I could not remember the details, only the feeling of being around family and a swarm of love.

As we drove out of town, I became aware of my parents and grandparents. I had that warm feeling again, the kind that shot right through me the night Mama died. I could imagine the four of them together, happy, peaceful. Whole and better than in real life.

All the anger of all those years started to dissipate, the bad times faded from memory, and all I was left with was the sound of my father's voice when he was happy, the way it cracked and went up like a boy's. And my mother's laughter, so genuine and full of momentary joy. And my grandmother's embrace, total, unconditional, and the sight of my grandfather's hair, sticking straight up like gray flames, and the quick dart of life that jetted out of his eyes, letting me know that though he was a man of few words, there was a lot of brain in that skull, neurons on full charge.

But the good feelings were again replaced by bad ones, and the roller coaster of grief continued. A few days after the funeral I got a cold. It turned into a flu, which led to bronchitis. My weight fell from 104 to 94 pounds. Philip thought I had an eating problem. But, I just ate less because I didn't have the energy. As I came to term with the grief, I slowly regained my appetite and my weight, but it took about a year.

There was much to regret when it came to my mother. I was ashamed because the main loss I felt wasn't her company, but the absence of how things should have been, how we would both have liked it to be. That's a loss you can't recover from.

She had been this frenzied squall in my life. My only defense against her cyclonic intensity of unarticulated misery was to stand back; all the way back to California.

A year after Mama died, Philip and I moved from San Francisco to Tiburon across the bay. I found a trail I liked and ran it often. The bay flanked me on one side and the verdant green of Marin County on the other. I thought about my family often when I ran, and sometimes I felt their presence. I had that warm sense again that they were somewhere looking down on me and pleased with the way I had turned out. I made decent money and I was married to a man I loved and who loved me. We had bad fights sometimes, but mainly things were good. He loved me unconditionally, the way my parents and my grandparents had. I can't say I had loved them unconditionally back, but then, I can't say that they deserved it all the time.

I haven't felt them near me in a long time. Maybe they have all been reborn. Mama's somewhere else now, perhaps, as a little baby. Down the street, maybe, is a boy, my father. They will meet and play their tortured love all over again, except this time it will be better. They'll still have problems, but not as many. Their heartache will be less. Somewhere in their lives will be my grandparents; maybe as neighbors or friends. I see Grandma as a doctor. Grandpa will be in communications because in his last life; he was so poor at it, grunting and mumbling his way through ninety-three years.

They will all be happier.

The only thing is I don't know where I will fit in. Maybe their souls are in limbo for now until my own life starts to wind down. I'll die and my soul will float to the next life. Maybe I'll be my parents' child again.

I'd like that, a second chance for us to get things right.

Printed in the United States
55867LVS00005B/122